A GIRL CALLED 51

by

ROGER CLARKE

Published by **CHIMERA**
ISBN 9781780807379

CHAPTER 1

Erica Pettinger loved to dance. She was very good at it and she knew it. She could pick up a rhythm and hold onto it, swaying her body sinuously, at one with the pounding beat of the club music. She was not bothered about the small crowd of young men who had gathered near *JoJo's* bar, swigging from their bottles of Becks and making ribald comments about her long legs or unfettered breasts.

She knew she looked good. Her long dark-brown hair, freshly washed and dried before she came out, only served to amplify the movements of her body. The shimmering dress, clinging like a second skin, promised much, and revealed what each flick of the skirt as she twirled was meant to. The UV lights picked up a brighter triangle front and back through the shimmer of the dress, where the shape of her tiny white thong showed through.

Hers was a deliberate ploy, to entrance, to make people want her and to not let them have her. She wanted to be untouched tonight. The last couple of times she had been to this club she allowed herself to be picked up by men who, under the light and quiet of the night, had not lived up to the promises made on the dance floor. They bored her. Tonight she had arrived with her friends from work and tonight she would leave with them.

Tony, the club's resident deejay, had noticed her too. But then he always had a few words for her. Tonight he singled her out during a particularly energetic techno number, encouraging her to gyrate to the beat so energetically and fluently that the crowd on the floor seemed to part to give her space, with several dancers giving up their own attempts so they could just watch her. And that made Erica worse. She loved being in the limelight, or any other light for that matter. She would have been happier as a television celebrity and fully intended to get there someday, someway, somehow. Her stepfather would help.

Erica was not very keen on her stepfather. Laurence Pettinger, MP. She did not like any politicians and being the daughter of a Member of Parliament caused people to make certain assumptions about her that she did not like. She wanted to be known as herself, not merely as his daughter. He had never been much of a father anyway, shipping her off to boarding schools and finishing schools and anywhere else he could dump her. As for her mother... well, they say behind every powerful man stands a powerful woman, except in their case it was difficult to see the join.

Mother was the ambitious one. Without doubt she wanted to be the Prime Minister's wife, but any hopes she had there had been dashed years previously when, in a vote for a new Party Leader, Laurence Pettinger had been eliminated at the first round. But it merely dented, rather than halted, her mother's ambitions.

Meanwhile, Erica decided it was her duty to rebel. They wanted her out of the way, so she did not interfere with or endanger their privileged position, which made her feel obliged to seek her own fame, rapidly becoming notoriety. The tabloid press adored her. She was seen out with footballers and music and film stars, pictured swinging her endless legs out of limousines as the cameras flashed.

Her denials of involvement with any of these men always carried a sparkle from somewhere behind her eyes, so that the interviewer was never quite sure whether she was serious or not. But most of all, any requests for 'a little more leg, Erica' were met with at least twice as much as she was asked for.

When her parents realised she could not - would not - be tamed, they sought to keep her profile as low as possible, which meant keeping her in petty cash. She was not above kicking up a storm if they denied her anything. Expense accounts with the best stores and membership of the trendiest clubs and casinos were all hers for the asking. And Erica asked... and asked... and asked again.

JoJo's was her favourite scene - for now. They indulged her too; knowing that sooner or later the press would latch on to her and along would roll some free publicity.

Occasionally she would hear her name spoken in hushed tones. 'Isn't that...?' voices would ask, never finding it necessary to complete the sentence. She intimidated some men; others saw her as a challenge. Erica did not care. She could pick and choose - and she did.

After the dance she joined her friends at a table on the low gallery. The surface was littered with bottles and glasses, some empty, some not even started. It was not unusual for men to send drinks over. They imagined it would buy them a piece of her, but she did not come so cheap. She needed a long drink after all the dancing, but the array of iced beverages at her seat were all her 'usual' - vodka and slimline tonic. She downed two glasses quickly, enjoying the cool liquid and prepared to wait for the kick of the alcohol.

Over the deafening noise she told Lisa, a blowsy blonde who she worked with and who trailed along with her occasionally, that she needed the toilet. Lisa was a secretary at the advertising agency owned by Nigel Hopcroft, a friend of Laurence Pettinger who, no doubt, had talked him into giving Erica the job in the first place, where he could keep an eye on her. She did not care about the job - it was a means to an end and nothing more. This was when she came alive. At night. Days were for ordinary people.

The two girls worked their way through the crowds, all too aware of the straying hands of so many men as they passed. Some she did not mind, some she found offensive and said so. She could cut a man dead with one glacial glance.

There was only one other girl in the toilets, repairing her hair in the mirrors. Erica and Lisa chose adjacent cubicles, chatting between them. They heard the door go as the other girl left, but they did not realise someone else had entered. Lisa, leaving her cubicle first, chatted brightly while Erica flushed the toilet. Then she stopped.

'Lisa?' Erica called, but apart from the muted thud of the base beat from the club there was nothing but silence. 'Lisa?'

She made sure her dress was as decent as could be and unlocked the cubicle door...

The shock stopped her calling out and, by the time she could react a strong leather-gloved hand was across her mouth and her arms were held from behind. She tried to kick out at a swarthy grey-faced man in front of her, but the one holding her anticipated the attempt and lifted her clear of the floor. A third man had a similar grip on the struggling Lisa, and a ball of cloth was stuffed into her mouth and held there with a band of surgical adhesive tape. While the man continued to hold Erica the other two quickly bound Lisa's wrists behind her and her feet together, pushing her back in the cubicle and taping her arms and legs to the toilet and cistern as Erica watched in horror.

Climbing up and leaning over the divider from the cubicle Erica had used, one man pushed the door to and bolted it. Then all three turned their attentions on Erica, one producing a bottle and a cloth pad from his pocket. She guessed that the sickly smell was chloroform, making her renew her futile struggles. As the cloth pad approached her mouth and nose the leather glove was lifted, but Erica did not have enough time to scream before the noise cut off. A few seconds later the world before her eyes started to melt into blackness.

CHAPTER 2

Erica's head pounded her awake. She knew it would hurt to open her eyes. She could not remember anything at first and thought she'd had a deep sleep, until the memories faded in. Still she thought she'd dreamt it all, but trying to move wrenched her into reality. Her legs were spread wide, as were her arms, each firmly secured to the four corners of a large bed with buckled leather cuffs attached to stout chains. She snapped her eyes open quickly, the pain from the glare sending sharp spikes into her mind. A heavy metal collar around her neck rattled chains as she moved, chains she could see were attached to the bed-head too, keeping her from rising more than a few inches from the mattress.

And she was naked.

Erica did not recognise the room at all. Light orange walls gave way to a pale cream ceiling. The furniture, or what she could see from her restricted position, looked expensive and classy. Dimmed wall lights provided all the illumination in the room - looking round she could see no sign of a window, just two heavy-looking doors leading to God-knew-where. On her left, beside the bed, stood a cabinet. Next to that was an upright chair. The right wall was made up mostly of mirrored wardrobe doors, with a circular table and three chairs in front of it. Between the doors stood a drawer unit, and directly above her watched the staring eye of a video camera.

'Help, let me out!' she called, struggling uselessly to pull her arms free. 'What do you want with me?'

The camera stared dispassionately back.

She tried calling a few more times, with similar lack of response.

'What do you want?' was a stupid question, she realised that. She was being held because of who she was. Or rather, as usual, who her stepfather was. She had no idea of how long she'd been there, nor even if it was day or night. The search would have started by now, she was sure of that. Even if they had not missed her, Lisa would have been found and raised the alarm. She thought about her parents making phone calls and mobilising the best police forces to find her; probably Special Branch for a politician's daughter, or at least a few detectives. Perhaps they were even raising the ransom to secure her release, ready for a dramatic exchange and the subsequent media circus that her mother would milk for all she could.

Her thoughts turned cold and clammy. How many times had her mother called her an embarrassment to Laurence's political aims? What if their daughter were found in a heap in some field somewhere, naked and battered? Or if she were never found? Her mother would tearfully appeal to the TV cameras, pleading for her release, but would she really want it? Would her stepfather get higher up the political ladder by harnessing the public's sympathy for his missing, possibly dead, daughter, who would never again embarrass them?

With a sick feeling in her belly Erica realised her mother could well sacrifice a pawn to protect the king.

'Help, let me out!' she tried again, looking into the camera's eye. She pulled and struggled until she had no energy left to pull any more. Then she started to sob, tears running down her face into the pillow as she asked, 'why, why, why?' over and over again.

They left her there for hours. Maybe they were watching, maybe not. She had no way of knowing. Then, for the first time since she'd come to, she heard sounds from beyond one of the doors, distant at first yet getting ever closer. She looked up as best she could as the door clicked and swung wide, allowing a girl about her own age to enter. The girl was blonde, her hair falling over her shoulders past the big metal collar around her neck, the attached chains going down each of her arms to leather cuffs, each secured in place with a small padlock. From there the chains continued to her similarly padlocked ankles. Unlike Erica, though, she was not naked; she wore a small lace bra, a thong and suspender belt, all in white, setting off black nylon stockings worn above black high-heeled shoes. The girl carried a bottle of mineral water.

The heavy door swung steadily closed and locks clunked mechanically into place.

'Help me,' Erica called, but the girl did not seem to hear her, giving no response or even looking at her. 'Where am I?' she tried again.

The girl simply walked to the side of the bed to place the tray on the bedside table before unclipping her collar and unscrewing the water bottle. She tipped the water to Erica's mouth and waited while Erica drank greedily.

'Why won't you speak to me?' Erica asked her desperately.

For the merest moment the girl's eyes made contact with her own and she

5

shook her head almost imperceptibly. All the time Erica tried to question her and all the time she refused to answer. When Erica got really frustrated the girl whispered, 'No talking.'

Suddenly a man's voice boomed out over a loudspeaker set somewhere in the ceiling. '36, I heard that!'

Fear overtook the girl's face as Erica watched. She closed her eyes in some terror Erica could only guess at.

'Stand at the end of the bed,' boomed the voice. 'And wait.'

Without hesitation the girl did as she was instructed, waiting, trembling, her eyes lowered. Less than five minutes later the door swung open again. Standing there was a man in a black shirt and jeans, a mask covering his eyes. He was a big man who almost filled the doorway as he stepped through it.

'Close the door,' he said to some unseen listener. His was the voice they had heard on the speaker.

The door swung mechanically closed and the locks clicked back into place. He ignored the girl at first, though she visibly cowered from his presence. Instead he walked over to Erica, looking her over before reaching a hand directly between her legs and pushing two fingers inside her.

'What the hell...?' Erica shouted. 'Get off me. Let me go!'

The man just smiled. 'You'll learn,' was all he said, his hands starting a journey over her body, feeling her breasts, hair, legs and back to her pussy, while she cursed and called him names, telling him in no uncertain terms what she would do to him when she got loose and how her stepfather would have him castrated. But all her threats did were to cause him ever more amusement.

'Like I said, you'll learn,' he said. '36!'

The girl snapped to attention.

'You did talk, didn't you? You may answer.'

'Yes, Master.'

'Any excuse?'

'No, Master.'

'Good, 36. There really was no use denying it. Now, we'll show 51 what obedience and punishment are all about, won't we?'

'As you command, Master.'

'What's all this 36, 51 crap?' Erica spat at him.

'You're new, so I'll explain,' he said calmly. 'Slaves don't have names here...'

'Slaves? What are you talking about - *slaves?*'

He ignored her question and carried on patiently. 'Slaves don't have names here. The first was called 1 - she's no longer with us, of course - and the next was called 2, and so on. Easy to grasp, no? You're the fifty-first. Nobody knows your name apart from the board, and nobody cares. You've ceased to exist as you were. You're 51 now, available for use by anyone who chooses to use you.'

'This must be some kind of sick joke.'

'I can see you need convincing,' he smiled at her. 'Very well. Prepare to be convinced. 36.'

'Yes, Master?'

'Suck her pussy.'

'Yes Master.'

Without hesitation the girl moved round to the side of the bed, climbing between Erica's legs and pressing her lips to Erica's pussy, dipping her tongue inside with practised skill.

'Get her off me!' Erica screamed, but the girl did not move away, just kept sucking until he told her to stop.

'Now kiss her.'

Erica moved her head to the side but the man's powerful hand gripped her chin, holding her still while the girl pressed her lips to Erica's, transferring her own taste with the kiss.

'Cease,' the man told her. 'Back to the end of the bed.'

Again the girl did not falter in her immediate obedience. The man let go of Erica's chin, walking over to a cabinet by the door. He pulled open a drawer and took something out. When he faced them again Erica saw it was a vicious-looking whip.

'Oh shit, no!' she cried.

'Lean forward, 36,' he said quietly.

Erica caught the girl's terrified eyes as she bent forward across the foot of the bed, placing her hands on the mattress between Erica's legs for support. The man stood a few feet behind her, the whip coiled in his grasp. He let the end fall on the floor, telling her to count aloud, and then drew the whip back before lashing out across the girl's buttocks.

36 screamed in pain. 'One...' she managed when her sobs had subsided sufficiently.

The cruel man worked at his own pace, only pausing to let 36 recover sufficiently to issue the count. It was so regular that Erica found herself tensing in anticipation and sobbing with the girl as each blow landed. It was impossibly inhumane and Erica could not understand how or why the girl could put up with it.

After the sob-wracked girl announced 'six' Erica could hold back no more. He'd made his point. It was time to stop.

'If you're trying to impress me you failed,' Erica said to him, and that made him stop. Walking round to the side of the bed again, that evil whip dangling from his grip, his dark eyes looked down on her from the holes in the mask. She was afraid; worried in case he used the whip on her.

'That was a foolish comment, 51,' he growled. He still watched her as he spoke over his shoulder to the sobbing girl. 'What will it mean, 36? Speak.'

'Six more, Master,' she said quietly.

'Louder.'

'Six more, Master.'

'That's right. I thought this would have taught you a little, 51, but you seem particularly stubborn. You have to realise that in this house you only speak when permitted to do so, or when a Master asks you a question and that any infractions, disobedience or rebellion will be severely punished. Your will has no place here and it will be broken. So your little outburst has earned 36 six more.'

'No, please, I'm sorry,' she pleaded.

'Unless you want to take her place?' he offered, cocking his head to one side as he stared down at her.

Erica looked beyond him to the sobbing girl, who slowly, unseen, shook her head. Erica stayed silent.

'I didn't think so,' he said at last, turning and resuming his position.

By the time 36 had uttered 'twelve' she was openly crying. The man walked to Erica again. 'Come here, 36,' he said.

As the girl arrived at his side he instructed her to turn. Erica's gaze fell on angry red lines cut into the girl's back and buttocks.

'This is what disobedience brings, 51,' the man continued in a matter-of-fact voice. 'The choice is yours. Obey and all will be well. Disobey and...' He left the sentence hanging in the air for a few moments before adding, 'We don't mind either way. We enjoy obedience, but we enjoy punishing too. So it's your choice. Have you anything to say, 36? Speak.'

'Thank you, Master,' she said immediately.

'For what, 36?'

'For whipping me, Master.'

'Good. Now, you may untie 51 and assist with her shower. For the purpose of instruction the pair of you may talk. It can be anything you want apart from personal details. Remember, we'll be listening. Any names, any background information, anything that could identify either of you will make the punishment you've just witnessed seem tame by comparison. If you want to talk about escaping, go ahead. That always amuses us.' He smiled at her before calling, 'Open the door.'

As the heavy portal swung silently open he turned and strode out. The girl made no attempt to escape through it; she just waited until it had closed again before breaking down into uncontrollable sobs.

'Can you untie me?' Erica asked her gently. 'Come on, please. I can help you.'

The girl sniffed and wiped the tears from her eyes with her hands, then moved to Erica to unfasten the chains from the leather wrist cuffs. When they were free she sat up to unfasten her own ankles, then pulled the girl towards her, letting her cry out her pain and misery into her shoulder, feeling the tears run down her skin. She had so many questions, but had to let the girl recover herself first. She made 'shhh' noises and told her everything would be okay. It was a ridiculous thing to say, since it was clear that all would not be okay, but gradually the girl's heaving sobs subsided and she was able to talk again.

'All right?' Erica asked.

The girl nodded.

'Who was he?'

'One of the Masters,' 36 told her.

'One of...? You mean there's more like him?'

'Oh yes, lots.'

'Are they all as cruel?'

'Some aren't. But some are worse.'

'Is that possible?'

'Oh yes, believe me, it's possible.'

Erica sensed laughter behind the camera's lens.

The girl faced her, speaking seriously. 'Please make sure you don't mention any names or where you lived or anything like that. It's forbidden and I can't take another whipping like that.'

'I'll try,' Erica assured her. 'Can you tell me how long I'll be kept here?'

'I don't know. Till they decide they've finished with you, I guess.'

'How long have you been here?'

'I'm not sure. We never see any newspapers or television or anything. You lose track of time.'

'Roughly,' Erica pressed.

'About two years, I suppose.'

Erica was flabbergasted. 'Two years? How can anybody keep someone hostage for two years? Surely people were looking for you?'

'Don't talk about that. We could slip up and mention our pasts.'

'What do they want? A ransom?'

'Oh no. There's no ransom. We're not hostages like that. We're here for their use.'

'Their use?' Erica felt uneasy.

'Yes, they all—'

A voice from the loudspeaker cut her off. 'That will be explained to her later,' it said. 'Change the subject.'

'What about our families?' Erica glanced nervously at the camera before adding, 'I mean, they'll have the police looking for us.'

'I don't know.'

'I read a book once, *The Story of O*. Have you read it?'

'Yes,' the girl replied. 'But she went to the chateau because she loved her man. We're here because they keep us here.'

'You're talking white slavery!'

'Call it what you like.'

'I can't believe this,' Erica said, shaking her head. 'I'll wake up soon, surely I will.'

'Just do what they say and you'll be okay,' the girl advised. 'It's pointless fighting them.'

'Just give in? Like that? That's like giving up on life.'

'Yes,' the girl said blandly.

'What about clothes and food and so on?' Erica asked, conscious of her nakedness and hunger.

'All provided for us. Most of the time it's stuff like this, but sometimes there

9

are more elaborate costumes. Sometimes they want us in uniforms.'

'What kind of uniforms?'

'The usual stuff. Nurses, harem girls, policewomen, teachers...'

'So we're like prostitutes?' Erica felt her anger rise.

'No, they get paid and get to go home after work.'

'What about a bathroom and the toilet?'

'Through there.' The girl waved an arm in the direction of the second door. 'All our rooms have one.'

'We get our own rooms?'

'Yes, this is yours. When they let you out you'll see your name on the door.'

'My name, or my number?'

'They're the same thing now.'

'Just how big is this place?'

'Massive. All of us have individual rooms, and then there are rooms for the Masters to stay in - much bigger than these, with double baths and jacuzzis and so on. There's the club and the restaurant and the gym and—'

'Do you know where it is?' Erica wanted to know.

'No, and they're very careful to make sure we don't find out.'

'Has anyone ever escaped?'

'They tell us nobody has,' 36 told her, an edge of doubt in her voice.

'If that's the case there should be 51 girls here.'

'No, some have been sold.'

Erica did a double take. 'Sold?'

'Yes, wealthy men can make offers to buy us.'

'This can't be happening,' she said incredulously, shaking her head in disbelief. 'Tell me this can't be happening.'

'But it is. There's nothing—'

The speaker boomed out again. 'Enough! Silence now.' The girl Erica only knew as 36 glanced up at the camera and stopped talking.

'I need the toilet,' Erica whispered.

'51,' the speaker said sternly, 'since you are new we'll make allowances, but not for very much longer. Silence means silence. You've already witnessed the penalty for disobedience.'

36 put her finger to Erica's lips, stopping any protest. She stood, beckoning with her hand to the second door. She pressed a small pushbutton that was set in the wall by its side, causing the door to swing open with the same mechanical precision as the main door. Inside, under the glare of bright white lighting, was a sumptuous bathroom, fitted in white and including a large bath, toilet, bidet, washbasin and separate shower cubicle. 36 beckoned her through.

'36, return to your quarters,' the speaker instructed. '51, enter the bathroom.'

Erica watched as the girl moved to the bedroom door and waited for it to open. Nothing happened.

'51, enter the bathroom,' the voice repeated. 'Enter the bathroom now!'

Erica sighed. There was no point in being too defiant yet. Her time would come. She took two steps forward into the bathroom. A few moments later she heard a click behind her. When she turned the door had shut, and there was no handle to open it again.

'How do I get out?' she called to the voice she was sure would be listening.

'No questions.'

She sighed heavily and lifted the toilet lid, watching herself in the mirror as she sat. She looked a mess, her hair limp and ragged, her makeup streaked. On the shelf under the mirror was a large array of cosmetics, a hairdryer, an electric toothbrush... everything she could need. Several brands were ones she used. Over the bath and in the shower cubicle stood a few bottles of shampoo, conditioner, bath oils and body gels. As her eyes continued to wander she glanced up, and another camera lens looked coldly down on her.

'God, isn't there any privacy here?' she demanded.

'You were warned, 51. Now you have earned a punishment.'

'Fuck you,' she muttered back.

She decided to take a shower. After all, there was nothing else to do. She tugged at the leather cuffs and their locks, but since they would not move she carried on into the shower wearing them. The water was warm and luxurious and after she'd washed her hair and cleaned off the remains of her makeup she started to feel human again. Two enormous fluffy bath towels completed the job, one to dry her and the other to wrap round her body while she sat to dry her hair. The temperature in the room was just right, but she decided to wear the towel to annoy the eyes behind the camera.

When she was dry she stood and faced the door. It opened inward, so there was no point in pushing and there was nothing to get a grip on to pull. She stared up at the camera impatiently. She wanted to give them a mouthful of abuse again, but with the memories of the other girl's whipping fresh in her mind she decided not to push too hard.

So she waited. And waited. And when nothing happened she sat on the toilet again.

'Take off the towel,' a woman's voice said eventually.

Erica did not move. She did not even look up at the camera, deciding instead to remove an imaginary piece of something from the corner of her eye.

'We can wait longer than you can,' said the voice.

Erica sighed heavily. She was not going to win this particular fight, so she stood and dropped the towel on the floor in an untidy heap. Immediately the door clicked and swung open, and when she moved back in her room she was surprised to see two people there. One was the girl known as 36, who sat on the furthest away of the three matching chairs that surrounded the small table to one side of the room. She did not look up as Erica walked in. The other occupant was a stern-looking heavyset man dressed in light slacks, a sweatshirt and the inevitable black mask, which did nothing to conceal the fact he'd lost most of his hair.

As Erica entered he beckoned her over to sit at the table opposite 36. The table in front of them was set for two, with bread rolls, a tureen of soup, cold meats and salad. A bottle of white wine rested in a pedestal-mounted ice bucket to the table's left.

'Eat,' the man's gruff voice told her. 'You may talk. Same rules, no personal details.'

This time the girls had no chance to do anything other than eat and make idle conversation while the man stood nearby to watch. Despite his presence the two girls talked about things that interested them, punctuated only by an occasional nervous glance at the man to make sure they weren't straying into forbidden topics. Erica told 36 that she liked to dance and was keen on tennis and badminton. 36 said she too liked badminton and perhaps they could play a match in the gym when she was settled in. Erica also learned the other girl was learning to speak French in the language room, responding to Erica's questions by telling her that they were encouraged to develop languages and social skills, and that all facilities were available within *The Complex*.

By the end of the meal, lubricated by the wine, both girls were starting to get along well, chatting freely and even sharing a few jokes while the stern man stood expressionless, his arms folded across his chest. They finished eating and took their time sipping the last of the wine.

Suddenly the man interrupted. 'Silence now. 51,' he barked.

'Me?' Erica said.

'Stand,' he said. 'Move over to the end of the bed. 36, follow her.'

Erica started to feel uneasy as he grasped her hand and roughly pulled her until she faced the bed. She struggled, expecting the worst.

'36, hold her other arm,' he growled.

Despite the fact the two females had been so friendly moments before, 36 did as she was told immediately, holding Erica's left wrist with both her hands, giving the man the freedom to fix one of the chains to the wrist cuff, pulling it tight enough that her knees touched the bed as she stood. Moving behind her he secured her right arm into position at the other side of the bed. Taking new chains from the drawer unit he knelt down by her right foot, which she tried to keep from his grasp, but he was far too strong. Fitting the chain to the clip on the cuff, he pulled until she had to move it towards the leg of the bed. Finally he treated the left ankle in a similar way, leaving Erica standing, legs parted, helpless.

'Please, no,' she begged the man.

'You were told to be silent, 51. You were told that defiance would be punished. Normally when you are whipped you'll be gagged, but today I want to hear you scream.'

Erica looked anxiously over her shoulder as he selected a whip from the drawer. It could have been the same one that had been used on the other girl; she had no idea.

'Do you like 36?' he asked her. 'Speak.'

'Yes, I do.'

'36, do you like 51?'

'Yes, Master.'

He offered the handle of the whip to the other girl. 'Whip her then. Hard.'

'Yes, Master.'

'I'll tell you when to stop. If I consider it's not hard enough I will take over and when I've finished, you will take her place. Understand?'

'Yes, Master.'

Erica turned to look at her new friend, who carefully avoided eye contact as she raised the whip, her wrist chains jangling as she brought it swiftly down.

The first cut was the worst pain Erica had ever experienced. She screamed out, begging for it to stop. 36 took no notice, raising the whip again and crashing its tail across Erica's rump. After four strokes Erica was sobbing, but nothing changed. No mercy was shown.

After two more she sagged forward onto the bed, but the target was still there and 36 still whipped it. Tears flowed down Erica's cheeks, dripping onto the bed-sheets below.

'Cease,' she heard the man say at last.

But it was only a temporary halt. Erica heard the drawer open again and a few moments later he was kneeling on the bed, attaching ropes to the rings in her collar. Pulling tight he attached one, then the other to something under the sides of the bed so her face was trapped, forced down against the mattress.

'Continue,' he told 36.

Almost immediately the whip cut across her again, hitting the upper parts of the backs of her thighs as she screamed into the bed. After two more strokes he called for a halt again, moving so she could see his eyes as he bent to talk.

'Do you still like 36?' he asked.

'Yes. She's not doing this. You are.'

'Still defiant, are we?' He smiled. 'It's going to be fun breaking you.'

'No, please, I wasn't being defiant—'

'Silence!' He paused for a few moments. 'Make no mistake, 51, it is 36 whipping you. I admit she's following orders, as you will before you know it. But there is a difference, and I'll prove it to you.'

Then he was gone. A few seconds later the whip lashed out again, snaking up the length of her back, a worse bite than any before. His face appeared in her blurred vision once more.

'Can you tell the difference?' He grinned. Erica nodded. 'Would you like to get your own back?' he asked. 'Would you like to whip 36?'

Erica shook her head. She could not do that. She just could not.

'Another day, then,' he mused. 'We'll save it for another day. But you will do it.' He rose and faced the other girl. '36, come here. Unzip me.'

He moved close to Erica's face, filling her vision with his torso as the other girl's hand opened his zip and withdrew a massive erection.

'Make me come, on her face,' he said.

Erica wished she could have turned away, but the one time she tried it he reached down to twist her back to face him, telling her that if she closed her eyes she would be whipped again. So she had no choice but to watch as 36's hand pumped ever faster up and down his shaft until after a few minutes he pushed his pelvis forward to spew a stream of sticky warmth all over her face and hair, roughly forcing her mouth open to take the last few spurts into her throat.

When he was finished he calmly zipped up. 'Oh, and one last thing,' he said to her. 'What's your name? Think very carefully how you answer.'

'51,' she said slowly, tears rolling down her cheeks to mix with the glutinous wetness he'd deposited there.

'Good. We knew you'd learn quickly.'

Without another word he turned and walked to the door, calling for it to be opened, then calling for 36 to follow him, leaving Erica helplessly fixed to the bed, the skin of her back, bottom and legs hot and raw and his semen running cold down her face.

CHAPTER 3

The next morning - at least Erica assumed it was morning, since she had been released, washed and fed after what seemed like hours strapped to the bed, then told to get some sleep - she had a visit from a woman.

Whoever she was Erica felt she had seen her before somewhere. She introduced herself as Emily. Her manner of dress - a tailored skirt suit and crisp white blouse - made it obvious she was not one of the numbered girls. She was older than Erica's twenty-four, probably by ten or twelve years. Her manner was ordinary, almost pleasant, such that Erica had to remind herself that she was still naked and being held against her will.

Emily invited Erica to sit on the same chair she had occupied while having the meal with 36 the day before, putting some papers and a clipboard on the table before taking the seat opposite.

'Now,' she said, smiling, 'I'm here to answer questions. I can't answer everything, but I'll tell you what I can. Ask away.'

'Where am I?'

'This building is known as *The Complex*. It is run to the standards of the best hotels in the world and has all the facilities you'll need. If there's anything you want that we don't have, you can ask at the proper time and the management committee will consider it. We meet every Friday. Next?'

'You still didn't say where we are.'

'No I didn't, did I? Let's just say we're in England and not near any towns or cities.'

'Why was I brought here?'

'As a slave.'

'A slave? Are you serious?'

'Absolutely serious,' Emily told her, making a note on her pad. 'You are here to satisfy the wants and desires of some very important people. You'll recognise some of them, I'm sure. Hence the need for absolute secrecy.'

'Why me?'

'Why not?' The woman looked her over casually. 'You're young, attractive, intelligent. You also have a fire which the Masters and Mistresses will enjoy taming.'

'How long will I be kept here?'

'Next question.'

'You didn't answer that one.'

'Next question.'

'Am I allowed out at all?'

'Oh yes. The grounds are vast. When you've been properly inducted you'll have daily exercise, including outside. And we have a full gym, a swimming pool, sauna, massage, jacuzzi. We also have some of the best chefs. If you have the right attitude you'll live a good life here.'

'Can I get a message to my friends and family?'

'No, unfortunately not.'

'Not even that I'm safe?'

'No.'

'What will I be expected to do here, for these so-called Masters?'

'Obey.'

'That's it? Nothing more specific?'

Emily smiled and put down her pen. 'Some of them have vivid imaginations. All you need to do is obey. If you do that you'll get along just fine. If you disobey you'll be punished.' She consulted a chart on her clipboard. 'I see you've had one whipping already.'

'Yes.'

'That was quick.'

'What if I escape?'

'You won't escape.'

'What if I try?'

'You won't escape. If you try you'll be punished.'

'My father will find me. He's an MP. He'll have the police find me.'

'We know who your father is.'

'Then you'll know he's a powerful man. He won't stop till he finds me.'

'He'll stop.'

Erica fell into an uneasy, disbelieving silence.

'Now,' Emily said after a few moments, 'you'll be comforted to know that all girls and all clients have compulsory medical checks - you had a thorough examination before you regained consciousness - so there's almost no risk of any unpleasant illnesses. Should you feel ill we have a doctor or nurse in residence twenty-four hours a day. Both are very experienced, so don't think trying to feign illness will get you anywhere. During your period you'll obviously not be as available as between, apart from those Masters who want you during that time.

Speaking is forbidden without permission. If you need to ask a question simply kneel on the floor with your head bowed and await permission to speak.'

'Are you serious?'

'You keep asking that, 51. And I keep telling you that I am completely serious. We'll try now. Stand.'

Erica stared at her.

'Don't be difficult, 51.'

Erica stood, following Emily's direction of how to kneel, sitting back on her haunches with her upturned hands resting on her thighs, her head lowered. She was told that she had to remain like that until given permission to speak. If such permission was denied she had to respond to whatever alternative instructions were given.

'How do I know who I have to obey?'

'All slaves wear chains and collars, or are otherwise secured. Dress varies depending on the occasion or the wishes of a Master, but usually you'll recognise fellow slaves. Just about anyone else must be obeyed.'

'Including you?'

'Including me.'

'I assume I have to have sex with these men.'

'And the women, if they want you.'

'But I'm straight,' she protested.

'That ceases to have any meaning here. You are what the Masters say you are.'

'I've no experience with other women.'

'You'll be trained.'

'Oh God, this can't be happening!' she sobbed.

Emily stood and moved next to her, a comforting arm round her shoulder. 'You'll soon get used to it, 51. It's not that bad a life if you obey.'

'I'm not 51, I'm Erica Pettinger,' she protested, but all the fight had drained from her.

Emily stiffened. 'Don't use that name. It's a punishable offence to use any name of any sort. You don't use your own name and you don't use a Master's name, even if you recognise him. Masters are referred to as Sir or Master, or in the case of women they are to be addressed as Ma'am or Mistress. Understand?'

'Yes,' Erica sniffed.

'Yes what? You may as well get used to it.'

'Yes, Mistress.'

'See? That wasn't so difficult, was it? Anyway, to move on, you'll be woken each day by the loudspeaker in your room. You will use the toilet, shower and wash your hair. All you need will be provided. Makeup courses are available if you need them, as are courses in deportment and social skills. All your clothes are also provided and will be laundered for you daily. The clothes for any particular day will be left on the end of the bed while you are showering. No variations in chosen clothing are permitted. You will remain in your room until called for. When you know your way about the place, you may be instructed to go somewhere on your own. Is all that clear?'

'Yes... Mistress.'

'Good. I think you'll do just fine. Anything else you want to ask?'

'Am I allowed to refuse anything at all?'

'No.'

'When do I have to start?'

'You've already started, 51. You're available for use right now. And I'll be the first.' Emily stood and pulled Erica to her feet. 'No words from now on. Come here,' she said gently, and reached up to cup her cheeks and move her lips to Erica's, giving her a deep, sensuous kiss which, despite her professed lack of experience, Erica found herself responding to.

'That's it,' Emily whispered. 'Kiss me back.'

Erica obeyed, kissing Emily full on the lips and responding to the invasion of the woman's tongue with gusto. Emily's hands started to roam down her back to her buttocks, causing Erica a sharp intake of breath as the hands brushed the wheals from her whipping. The hands moved on, seeking her breasts, cupping them, the thumbs teasing her nipples erect. Emily dipped her head and sucked each rigid bud in turn, drawing them into her mouth to flick them with her tongue.

Erica felt awkward. Her hands wanted to push away and at the same time pull the woman closer, but she was not sure what was allowed.

'Undress me,' Emily breathed, and then in a louder voice called out, 'camera off.'

Erica reached for the buttons on Emily's jacket, unfastening from the top one, two, three, before pushing the jacket off her shoulders, laying it on the table. Emily renewed the hungry kiss while Erica unfastened her blouse buttons, fiddling with the cuffs until it too lay on the table. The black bra was impressively filled, pushing upwards to give a tanned, succulent cleavage. Emily unfastened it herself, letting it fall to the floor before pulling Erica's mouth down to her breasts. To Erica's surprise she took to suckling the woman's nipples easily, and in different circumstances would have enjoyed it. Emily was definitely enjoying it, moaning each time Erica flicked her tongue or kissed a particular way. 'Keep going,' she breathed.

Despite her situation Erica sensed that if she kept in with this woman, gained her trust perhaps, it could give her an edge, so with that motivation she added a determination to her actions, kissing her breasts and nipples while moving her hands to the fastening of the skirt, pushing it over her bottom, over the inevitable suspender belt and letting it fall to the floor.

Emily pushed her away for a moment. 'Go to that drawer,' she said, her voice cracked and breathless. 'There'll be a dog leash there. Bring it to me.'

'Yes, Mistress,' Erica said, pleased she was having an effect and determined to capitalise on it. She walked to the drawer and opened it, sorting through the array of harnesses, whips and restraints until she found the leash, carrying it back to Emily. The woman took it, fixing the clip to Erica's collar, wrapping the loop round her hand and pulling Erica to her knees. Once there she wrapped the leash several times round her right hand and pulled Erica's face to her crotch. Erica could feel her warmth even through the silk French knickers she wore.

'Ever sucked a woman, 51?'

'No, Mistress.'

'Take off my knickers.'

Erica reached up to Emily's waist, pulling down, watching as the suspender belt and then the dark-brown patch of hair came into view, and then continuing to lower them past her dark stockings. Emily lifted her feet to step out of them, kicking her skirt aside in the same movement.

Emily gripped the leash and pulled her in, reinforcing the movement with a hand on the back of Erica's head as she parted her thighs and tilted her pelvis forward. Erica accepted the inevitable in as detached a way as she could, at first kissing the hair, then as the older woman pushed forward, directly between her labia, which opened from the movement, coating Erica's lips with warm, tangy honey. Emily bucked and trembled.

'Oh, that's good. Lick now, use your tongue.'

Erica had tasted herself in the past, experimenting at home in her teens and sometimes on the cocks of men friends who thought she should like them pulling out of her just before they came, to push into her mouth and ejaculate there. Emily's taste was similar. No big shocks. She reached behind to grip Emily's buttocks as she pressed her mouth in.

'Oh yes, you're good, you're really good,' Emily was saying from somewhere above her.

With some effort Emily broke the connection and walked towards the bed, yanking on the leash to pull Erica to a kneeling position beside it.

'Stay there,' she ordered, going back over to the chest to open the second drawer. After a few moments sorting through she returned with two vibrators, which she placed on the bed. Reaching for a thin one she moved it to Erica's mouth, telling her to lick it well before moving behind. Erica felt its coldness touch her buttocks and then slide between. Emily moved it downwards, not to her pussy but to the rosebud of her anus, pressing steadily. Erica gasped and winced as it opened her up, meeting some resistance. A sudden vicious slap across her buttocks made her yelp and must have caused her to relax, because before she realised what had happened Emily pushed the slim plastic phallus all the way home.

'Comfy?'

Erica shook her head.

'You'll soon get used to it. You'll have to learn to relax. Most of the Masters will want to fuck you there.'

'I'll try, Mistress,' she offered.

Emily reached for a bigger vibrator and slid it effortlessly into Erica's pussy, meeting no resistance. Erica was surprised how wet she was. Then the older woman pulled her upright to a kneeling position so she could mount the bed, her legs wide. She grabbed the leash and pulled Erica's face back in.

'Suck,' she gasped. 'Suck me.'

It took only a few moments before Emily exploded, pulling Erica's face into her cruelly, uncaring whether she was able to breathe or not, bucking and rubbing and riding out her orgasm. Erica, meanwhile, just allowed her head to be pulled where Emily wanted, feeling the intrusion of the two objects inside her as she was twisted this way and that.

Eventually Emily settled back, smiling dreamily and covered in a thin sheen of sweat. 'Good, 51. You did well. I can see you'll be popular here. Don't stop; just be gentle for a while.' She settled back while Erica lazily licked and kissed.

She wanted some for herself now, incredibly turned on regardless of the fact she was with another woman. But she suspected asking for her own satisfaction was a bad idea and wondered if masturbation after Emily had left would be permitted.

Emily gradually started to come back to the present, responding with moans as Erica's tongue and lips roused her once more. 'Stand up,' Emily told her. 'Turn around.' When Erica had done so the woman pulled her hands behind her back and fastened her wrist cuffs together with the spring clips. 'Now do it again,' she said. 'Make me come again.'

She did not hold the leash this time, leaving Erica to dictate the pace and the pressure. Some kind of experiment, Erica imagined. Well, she was not about to fail such a transparent test. She licked and kissed keenly, twirling her tongue around Emily's clitoris, sucking the bud, drawing it into her mouth and taking the older woman closer and closer to her second climax.

'Oh yes, lick, suck! Oh!' Emily certainly was not quiet when she came, and after one final convulsion she roughly pulled Erica's head clear, pushing her back hard enough that she fell on the floor, then lay back, gasping heavily. 'God, I needed that!'

Erica's lust and needs were powerful after her exertions too, so she struggled to her knees and sat back on her haunches, head lowered, her hair falling down and covering her half-closed eyes. She waited.

Emily, still recovering from her second orgasm, noticed the change of mood and Erica's sudden stillness.

'You want to ask something?' she said, leaning up on her elbows. 'Speak.'

'I need to come.' Erica hated herself for giving in so easily to her lust. 'Mistress,' she added, hating herself even more. 'Please.' The two vibrators, sitting lifelessly within her, teased without satisfying.

'Very well,' Emily smiled, then stood up and moved to the drawer unit once more. When she turned back she was carrying some kind of harness, unfastening buckles and straps as she walked. As Emily stepped into the strap-on dildo and started to fasten it Erica saw, to her surprise, not one but three black plastic penises bobbing from it. Fascinated, she watched as Emily pushed one deep inside herself, her eyes closing as she enjoyed the penetration. That left two sprouting up in front of her when the harness was strapped in place; and Erica did not need it spelling out where those were going.

Despite the fact she had never had anal sex, the vibrator lodged inside her rectum had made her want to try it, so she did not have the same dread she perhaps would have had if the strap-on were her first introduction. Men had wanted it from her before but she always refused, even throwing a couple out of her apartment for trying.

Emily pulled her face to the dildos, telling her to suck, explaining that it would ease their passage into her. She did her utmost to coat them with saliva. Emily pushed her forward so the upper part of her body was flat on the bed, her bound arms held uselessly behind her, before easing both vibrators from her and dropping them onto the bed. The older woman knelt between Erica's legs and eased forward, positioning the phalluses at both of her entrances before pushing slowly, steadily, painfully, within her.

Erica held her breath, not knowing whether she wanted to push back towards Emily, thereby forcing the dildos further inside, or to pull away, to resist. It was a battle of comfort versus lust. Lust won easily. Erica pushed, Erica wanted, Erica got.

Finally Emily was as far inside her as it was possible to be, staying still so both of them could feel this deepest of penetrations. She started to move, slowly, then gradually faster, taking hold of Erica's hair, pulling herself in, pumping forward and back. Erica gasped and squealed.

'Silence!' Emily hissed, and without stopping her thrusting she picked up one of the vibrators, pulling Erica's head back so she could push it in her mouth. 'I said silence,' she growled. 'Suck on that, slave!'

Erica had no idea which of the vibrators she was sucking on and cared even less. She would have sucked anything right then. She would have done anything. She was more excited than at any time she could remember and she was being taken rapidly, urgently, screamingly to orgasm. No choices, no decisions. And right along with her, riding the other end of the dildo, Emily had her third.

Her aim had been to ingratiate herself with Emily but she had to admit - to herself, nobody else - that she enjoyed sex with the woman. And she thought she'd won her over too; at least until both had recovered.

'One last thing, 51,' Emily said as she finished dressing. 'Do you think I'm stupid? Speak.'

'Er... no, Mistress.'

Emily moved across and roughly twisted her face towards her. 'You thought you could manipulate me, didn't you? Thought you could get my trust by playing along?'

'No, I—'

'Silence! You're an object, 51, a slave to be used and cast aside. You're trash. Get used to it.' She stood and collected her papers. 'Camera on.'

'My name's Erica,' she protested softly.

'What?'

'Erica. It's my name.'

Emily walked swiftly across, viciously slapping her across the face. 'You are 51. You have no name.'

'Fuck you,' Erica spat, her cheek already reddening from the harsh blow.

Emily put her papers on the bed and pushed Erica's head down next to them, pulling the leash down to an eyelet on the side and tying it there. 'Okay,' she said sourly. 'Have it your way.' She looked towards the camera.

'Set up our special initiation for 51,' she called, and then pulled Erica's face towards her once more. 'You will learn, 51, no matter how long it takes.'

Emily walked to the door, which clicked and swung open as she approached, then swished closed after she departed.

CHAPTER 4

By the time they came for her she ached. Her hands, still clamped behind her, needed movement, and the fact her head was pulled hard down to the bed meant she had to stay kneeling. She tried straightening her legs a few times, but the collar nearly strangled her as her body dropped. She even tried getting up on the bed, but the leash was too tight to allow it.

Time went very slowly. She was not fed, although another girl, one she'd not seen before, came in a few times and gave her water from a feeder bottle. Thinking she had little to lose now she tried talking to the girl, but did not get a single word in return.

They arrived noisily, entering the room and moving behind her. Emily was there, giving orders, and there were two men wearing the masks she had already seen. Three girls followed them in, each wearing similar black lacy underwear, stockings and heels, each shackled with the same loose chain arrangement fastening their necks to their wrists to their ankles, just as 36 had worn before.

Erica was frightened, wishing she had not pushed her luck with Emily. 'Mistress, I'm sorry,' she started, but from behind her a swish coincided with sudden pain in her buttocks. She had no idea who had hit her, nor with what; all she knew was it hurt.

'Too late, 51. It's easy to obey when you're scared, isn't it? But you have to learn to obey all the time, without question.'

'I will, Mistress.'

'Silence!'

Erica screamed as she was hit again. Male hands unfastened the leash and her cuffs, pulling her roughly to her feet. The same hands quickly unlocked the leather cuffs, replacing them with heavy metal ones, clipping her wrists to her collar by a few short inches of chain. Her ankles were shackled together, so the only steps she would be able to take would be short ones.

Emily led the party through the open door. The two men, who stayed in close attendance behind her, pushed Erica along immediately behind the woman she'd had such pleasure with shortly before. She could feel their eyes on her naked buttocks as she walked. The three silent attendants followed them, the clinks of their chains drowned by the clatter of the heavier ones on Erica's ankles.

The corridor outside could have been in a plush hotel, the Hessian above the dado rail punctuated by ornately-framed paintings every few feet. The heavy wooden doors at each side carried plaques inscribed with numbers, so she guessed each room was much like hers, home to another prisoner of the regime who had stolen her liberty. Erica resolved to be strong, to hang on to her name, to be the one who liberated the slaves. They would not break her.

At its midpoint the corridor branched off to the right. This passageway looked similar to the one she'd been awkwardly shuffling along, but it was much busier. In the distance she could hear the general murmur of conversation and now and again someone would move quickly from one door, or into another, most activity coming from double doors at the end of the passage. Erica smelled food, tugging at her hunger.

As they neared the double doors a slave girl came out from one to their left, stopping immediately as she saw the entourage, standing with her head bowed until they passed.

The doors swung open automatically in to the restaurant. Inside were perhaps thirty tables, almost all occupied by diners. By far the majority were men, but a few elegantly dressed women were sprinkled around. One table was all female, with three attractive women sipping white wine and chatting. Their entry into the hall produced a noticeable lull in the conversation, most heads turning to watch their progress towards a raised, curved platform at the far end of the hall. Erica heard a male voice say, 'Here's the floor show,' as she passed.

The two men beside her took an arm each to march her to the stage, stopping before a circular plinth that had two stout vertical posts set into it. She was quickly unshackled before her arms were roped to the tops of the two posts and her legs drawn apart to be tied by ropes at the bases, such that she formed an X shape. Once she was secured the men left her there alone, under the gaze of probably a hundred or so diners and under the unforgiving glare of coloured spotlights.

As her eyes became accustomed to the lighting she was able to look out over the room. The girls were dressed in the same kind of underwear she had become used to seeing, yet without the chain arrangement, which she assumed would impede their waitress duties. Apparently each table had its own exclusive girl who served the food and wine, attendant to the diners' every need. Erica noticed that it was quite common for the diners to touch the girls, caressing buttocks, legs and breasts. Occasionally someone would remove an item of clothing, so that the girl had to continue topless or without the thong.

A commotion over to Erica's right, where a girl dropped and smashed a dish, saw the poor culprit bent across the lap of one of the male diners and spanked to the enthusiastic cheers of the surrounding guests.

Erica could not even begin to guess what this place was. During the next hour or so, as she stood naked and helpless on her podium, she watched the scene before her, the busy waitresses entering and leaving from the swing doors almost directly opposite her; the noisy diners with their clinking glasses and ribald laughter; the ever-present masked men keeping a supervisory eye on everything that happened.

For the first time since she got here she could see fading daylight beyond sliding full-length windows, to the right of the kitchen doors on the far wall. A paved patio gave way to a grassy slope that disappeared into the diminishing light.

Her eyes snapped back to the doors at the far end as they opened again for another party of diners. Erica recognised the heavyset man immediately, though she could not remember why at first. She searched her memory for clues and finally it came to her.

His name was James and she did not like him. She had seen him not six weeks beforehand, at her house in Surrey. She had recognised him then, too, from his frequent appearances on the television, interviewing politicians who squirmed under the onslaught of unwanted questions. She remembered that several times during his visit she had caught him looking at her, but when she met his eyes he had not looked away as most men did. He kept on looking deliberately at her body, giving her the uneasy feeling he wanted her. But apart from that he'd been pleasant enough and she'd been pleasant back.

She kept her eyes on him, waiting for a chance to make contact. He could get word to her parents, if only she could get word to him.

Time passed and Erica started to feel tired, the ropes stretching her limbs. She was almost grateful when a tall, silver-haired man took the stage and flicked on a microphone, taking it from its stand and calling for attention.

'Ladies and gentlemen, as most of you know we have a special item this evening. An initiation.' He walked across to Erica and looked her in the face. 'What's your name, slave?' He held the microphone out towards her.

The diners watched, all perfectly silent. Someone coughed at the rear of the hall. This was her chance and she had to take it. If she could make James realise who she was, that would start the ball rolling towards her freedom.

'I am Erica Pettinger, daughter of the MP Laurence Pettinger. I'm being held here against my will. Can somebody get word to my parents?'

The silence remained for a few seconds, to be replaced by mounting laughter.

'I'm Erica Pettinger!' she repeated desperately over their noise. 'Please... can somebody get word to my parents?'

The man took the microphone away and spoke. 'You see, ladies and gentlemen, we have another fighter. You'll excuse me if you have to do without your slaves for a few minutes? Slaves, to your positions.'

Erica watched as the girls put down whatever they were carrying and moved towards the platform, kneeling on the carpeted floor just beyond the curved front with an ordered efficiency that told Erica it was not the first time they had done this. When all thirty-two girls were kneeling, heads bowed, the man spoke again.

'What's your name?' he asked her, offering the microphone for her reply.

'Erica Pettinger.'

He moved to one of the kneeling girls.

'What's your name, slave? Speak.'

The girl did not hesitate. '27, Master,' she said quietly.

'No, I mean your real name.'

'I have no other name, Master.'

'Good.'

He repeated the exercise with three other girls, including 36, the girl Erica had first met, then returned to face her.

'You see, 51? You're the odd one out here. You insist you have another name. You think you can rebel. You think you can beat us. What you don't realise is that the Masters and Mistresses here are quite happy for you to be defiant. They will enjoy seeing you broken. Keep us informed of your name, won't you?'

'I'm Erica Pettinger,' she hissed, staring him in the face.

He smiled and picked up a remote control from a holder on the wall. The circular plinth clicked into motorised life, rotating until Erica was facing the rear wall, her back to the diners. The murmur of expectant conversation had started again.

'27,' the man called. 'Fetch the whip.'

Erica watched as the girl stood and moved to a cupboard along the same wall she faced, opening it and taking out a single-tailed whip that rested on a blue velvet cushion, reinforcing the ceremonial feel about what was happening. She quickly returned, bowing her head and offering the whip to the man.

He put down the microphone and moved to a point behind Erica and to her left. Erica waited, tensing for the inevitable. The man waited too, choosing his moment. Erica could only tense for so long before she needed to take a breath. As she did so he lashed the whip across her back. She screamed, arching against the blow.

The man did not strike again. He picked up the microphone. 'Your name?' he asked her.

'Erica!' she spat.

He smiled. 'You are splendid sport,' he said. 'We're taking bets,' he announced to the diners.'

During the excited hubbub that followed he approached Erica and spoke quietly, the microphone switched off. 'Do you know what the betting is for?' he asked rhetorically. 'It's for how many you take before you break, 51.'

'Go to hell,' she hissed.

The sting of the first lash still hurt her back as she waited for more. Emily went to each table in turn, making notes. When the betting was concluded the silver-haired man called for quiet again.

'Right, ladies and gents, I think we're ready.' He walked across the front of the stage, looking down on the pretty lowered heads. 'We'll start this end. Number 2, step forward.'

Erica watched as the girl on the far right stood, taking hold of the offered whip.

Her naked breasts bobbed as she stepped up on the podium. With mechanical efficiency she raised the whip and brought it down hard across Erica's back. While Erica screamed and pulled at the ropes the girl handed the whip back to the man and approached her, saying in a clear voice, 'What is your name?' The man held the microphone close by to hear her answer.

'E-Erica,' she sobbed. The girl resumed her place below the stage.

'Next!' barked the man.

The pattern was the same for each girl. She would take the whip, lash out, hand back the whip and ask the question, while the man held the microphone to capture every question, every answer, every cry and every scream. There was no suggestion of regret, remorse or sympathy from any girl. Each time Erica screamed out and each time she replied to the question with her own name. By the eighth girl she was crying desperately.

'Erica, Erica, Erica, Erica,' she babbled incoherently, the ropes taking most of her weight now. Then the next girl stepped forward.

'Please, no more, please, I'll say it!' she cried out, but nobody took any notice. The next girl struck just as savagely as the others had, but when she asked the emotionless question she got a different answer.

'51,' sobbed Erica. 'My name is 51...'

Her mumbled acknowledgement echoed around the room, picked up and amplified by the sound system. A ripple of applause grew. Someone whistled.

'Again,' said the man, bringing the microphone close.

'51... my name is 51.'

'Good,' he smiled. 'That wasn't so difficult, was it? The score is nine, ladies and gentlemen.' He looked across at the next girl, standing ready to take her turn. 'Continue,' he said, handing her the whip.

'No, please no!' Erica shrieked, realisation dawning. 'I said what you wanted. Please stop, I beg you. I'll do anything.'

'That's right, 51, you will do anything. And you'll start by enduring this punishment. You must realise we punish when we want to, because we have a reason or because we don't. It's not yours to question, only to endure. Continue!'

So Erica was whipped by all the girls, sobbing and screaming until she hung loosely from her bonds, sweat coating her body. When her ordeal was over the girls were instructed to return to their duties, but Erica was not released. She had become a showpiece, a symbol of the futility of resisting against impossible odds. As people finished their meals some came up on the podium and looked at her back, or her nakedness. Some touched, invaded her body. A harsh-looking woman in black went behind her and drew her tongue up her spine, moving round so Erica could see the disdain in her face. A man brought a salt cellar to sprinkle on her wounds, laughing cruelly as her screams started again.

Gradually fewer and fewer people remained. As the diners left their girls went with them, though Erica could not guess where. She had been looking for her stepfather's friend, James, hoping against hope that he could be her salvation.

He was still in the room, drinking brandies with his three associates. Erica watched over her shoulder as they finally stood, his friends leaving the room as he approached Emily and spoke words Erica could not hear. Then both walked towards the platform.

'Not so haughty now, are you, 51?' he smiled. 'I remember you, in case you wondered. I remember how you looked at me, too. Such an arrogant look. But we're not so arrogant now, are we? Turn her round.'

Emily pressed the button on the remote until Erica was facing the man. He was already taking off his jacket. As the plinth shuddered to a halt he started to unbutton his shirt.

'No, please no,' Erica cried, weakness preventing her from putting any fight into her tone.

'No talking,' he said gently. 'Just accept your fate. If you say a word I will have you whipped again.' He paused to let the threat sink in; he knew she could take no more.

'I know you saw me earlier and I know you hoped I'd somehow rescue you. I could see it in your eyes, even from there. But I don't want to rescue you. I want to use you. I want to pay you back for that arrogant teasing at your parents' house. It's more fun that I know you.'

He did not stop until he was naked, Emily's eyes flicking between his erection and Erica's face.

'Take her down, please,' he ordered Emily.

They untied her feet first. As her arms were freed she sagged, all strength evading her, so that Emily had to support her. James stepped forward to help lower her to the floor, onto her hands and knees. She guessed what was coming, but she had no strength left to resist.

James looked down on her beaten back as he kicked her legs apart and knelt between them. Even through her exhaustion and discomfort she was surprised how easily he slid into her.

'No words, slave?' he taunted as he started to pump at her.

Erica was too exhausted to answer. James showed no concern about her whatsoever, holding her hips to stop her collapsing altogether as he worked himself to a rough, thrusting climax deep within her body, with Emily looking on. When he was spent he let her go, so that she slumped forward onto her front.

Emily crossed to a phone on the wall. 'Right, you can clear away now,' she said quietly, placing the phone back on its hook before kneeling to pull Erica's head up by her matted hair. 'What's your name, slave?' she asked.

'51, Mistress,' Erica gasped.

'Do you have any message for your parents?' James asked.

Even through her exhaustion Erica was not going to fall for that one. They had their victory. Erica had nothing left with which to fight.

'I have no parents, Master,' she managed to murmur.

Two men in black masks appeared on the stage, picking her up as if she weighed nothing. One folded her over his shoulder in a fireman's lift, quickly carrying her through the restaurant as other girls cleared away dishes and set the tables anew. All of them completely ignored her. Why not? She had become a number, just like them.

People were still milling about in the corridors on the way back to her room. Some stopped the man who carried her, wanting to examine the welts or her hopeless exposure. Eventually they arrived back at her room, where the man lowered her onto the bed, not saying a word as he retraced his steps and left.

The door swung silently closed as the camera stared coldly down on a broken young woman.

CHAPTER 5

During the night Erica was given unexpected medical attention, bathing and dressing her wounds with uncharacteristic gentleness. The male doctor and the female nurse who attended her made comments about her condition, told her what to do, tended her carefully. The one thing they did not do was ask her opinion about anything.

Erica assumed, for safety's sake, that she was not allowed to speak to them either. She wished they would gag her or something, because it was natural to want to speak and required great self-discipline to stay silent.

In the morning the doctor's visit was accompanied by another silent girl, a pretty blonde who could not have been more than eighteen and who was dressed, as expected, in her uniform of just underwear and stockings. She pushed a trolley containing coffee, croissants and a selection of cereals.

'I'm permitted to ask if you prefer tea,' the girl said, before adding, 'and you're permitted to answer.'

'No, coffee's fine,' she told the girl, who quickly turned to leave.

Erica's natural instinct was to ask who she was, but she swallowed the urge quickly. She watched the girl retreat, her eyes drawn to where the thong disappeared between her buttocks. She needed to know whether the other girls received beatings on a regular basis and how severe they were, but there were no recent marks on this pert derriere. But to her surprise, then mounting horror, she noticed something else.

On the lower part of the girl's right buttock she could clearly see the number 42 etched into the skin. The girl had been marked with a permanent tattoo to remind everyone that she was nothing more than property.

Erica felt nauseous. Would that be her fate too, or had this just been to punish another rebellious inmate? She wanted to bury the thought, to run, to escape, to pretend this was not happening. But she knew this was no dream, the imprints of last night's pain saw to that. So she had to know, had to ask.

Erica struggled from the bed, wincing as the movements stretched her tortured skin. The nurse looked up, glancing at the open door, ready to move if she made an attempt to escape. But Erica was too exhausted to even think of that. She got off the bed and sank to her knees, lowering her head and placing her upturned palms on her thighs.

The doctor faced her. 'You want to ask something? Speak.'

'That girl, the one who left, has she been tattooed?'

'Yes,' he said, totally matter-of-fact.

Erica swallowed hard. 'Will I be too?'

'Of course. All the girls are.'

Erica felt the nausea overtake her. From somewhere deep inside the contents of her stomach rose. She went dizzy, her body convulsing.

'Quick, get her to the bathroom,' he told the nurse. 'Hold onto it, put your hand over your mouth.'

Erica knew his concern was more for the carpet than for her. But she held on until she made the bathroom, sinking to her knees and heaving into the toilet while the nurse held her shoulders. She felt cold, her skin wet with a slick of fresh perspiration.

'It's not so bad,' the nurse said to her.

'Have you had it done?' Erica had to ask.

'Camera off,' she called out, waiting for a few moments before speaking again. 'No, but I've been there when it's been done.'

'Why are you all so cruel?' Erica asked.

'Money and power, that's what it's all about.'

'What is this place?' Erica asked.

'It's better that you don't ask questions like that.'

Erica sat back on the floor as the nurse handed her a towel. 'When will I get done?'

'When they decide.'

'You're not one of them, are you?' she asked.

'I'm an employee here,' the nurse told her. 'So no, I suppose I'm not one of them.'

'How do you put up with it?'

'It pays five times what I could earn anywhere else, that's how.'

'What do your friends and family say?'

The nurse looked nervously around. 'I don't tell them. I'm sworn to secrecy. Even my husband doesn't know what I do; he just thinks it's some secret government job. If I told anyone... well... I won't. Quiet now,' she said hastily, as though she had already said too much.

'Please tell me, who are they?'

'Politicians, judges, doctors, film and TV people... anyone with enough money to keep the place going. Now quiet. Camera on!'

The nurse helped Erica to her feet and back out into the room, where the doctor waited. The nurse helped Erica into bed, clipping a chain between her collar and the bed-head.

Erica lay back and tried to sleep as the nurse and doctor left the room. Whoever was watching cared enough to dim the lights.

Erica's sleep did not come easily. Every time she moved she felt a stab of pain, and even when she did doze she would have terrifying nightmares of men and women with tattooing implements, and two numbers that when held together made her number - 51.

Other people attacked her with whips and lashes. Every so often she would see her mother or stepfather in the background trying to get through the lines of people, but never able to make it. In her dreams she called out to them, but every time they got close she was pulled further away. She awoke with a scream, trying to sit upright but immediately pulled back by the chain.

She had no idea how long she had slept or what time it was. Within a few minutes the door opened and the nurse was back, accompanied by a blonde woman pushing another trolley of food. She was dressed the same as all the others, but was older, at least in her mid-thirties. Erica's eyes darted to her bottom as she turned. Just below a line of fading purple stripes she could make out the number 6. She waited silently as the nurse checked Erica over, and then left.

'We're allowed to talk,' she said quietly. 'I'm 6.'

'I'm 51,' Erica said, cursing herself for not being stronger.

'You should eat, you need strength. There's enough for both of us. I'll set it on the table.'

Erica ruefully fingered the chain at her throat. 'I can't, unless you have a key.'

'Er... no.' The woman smiled, then looked up at the camera and sank to her knees in the required position.

Nothing happened. The woman waited. Several minutes passed in silence. Eventually the loudspeaker's cold voice rang out.

'You want to ask something, 6?'

'May 51 be unlocked, Master?' she said. 'So we can eat at the table?'

'Yes. Set the table. Someone will come along with a key.'

The blonde got to her feet and smiled. 'See, it's easy if you know what to do.'

'You're the sixth one here?' Erica asked.

'That's me. There's only one girl who's been here longer, number 4.'

'What happened to the others?'

'Sold, I imagine,' she replied. 'Obviously I'm not attractive enough.'

'I don't believe that,' Erica told her. 'You're really lovely.'

'Thank you. But for whatever reason I'm still here.'

'How long have you been here?'

'I wish I knew. With no newspapers, TV, or even clocks, it's difficult to tell. I'd guess between six and ten years.'

'What?'

'It's not so bad. I didn't have that much of a life before and here I get all my meals, all my clothes, a roof over my head, sports facilities, the best medical attention... pretty much anything I want, really.'

'Except your freedom.'

'I'm not unhappy,' she said simply.

'Don't you miss your family?'

The loudspeaker's voice immediately came on. 'Don't answer that, 6. You have no family. You have no past.'

6 shrugged and smiled.

Just then the nurse returned and unlocked the chain connecting Erica to the bed.

'What about the sadism?' Erica asked when she had gone and the door closed again.

'I do as I'm told. The only beatings I get are when people get off on beating me. Some of the Masters are very generous. Some are quite gentle too.'

Erica had a feeling this woman had been planted on her to sell the place. If she was for real she had given up on freedom, on liberty, on life itself. If she was mid to late thirties and she had been here for the time she suggested, then she could have had a husband, even children.

Yet Erica knew she would get no answers that would be permitted. And she had no desire to inflict more pain on the woman. She ran through the idea in her mind. What if she did have children and one day she was just taken away and told to pretend they did not exist? And what about the kids themselves? Were they still out there, searching for their mother?

'Do we ever get to see daylight?' Erica asked.

'Yes, if you want to. We have exercise in the grounds.'

'Why don't you escape?'

The woman cast an uneasy glance at the camera above the bed, which had moved across to point right at them. She waited; expecting to be forbidden to answer, but no sound came from the speakers.

'Nobody escapes.'

'Change the subject,' boomed the loudspeaker.

'Yes, Master,' 6 said quickly.

The loudspeaker boomed out again, its deep male voice resounding into the room. Whoever was monitoring the conversation was clearly getting bored. 'Both of you stand in the centre of the room. Face each other.'

6 was quickly in position. Erica took longer, still finding movement an effort, especially when she had been still for a while. She moved to stand facing the older woman.

'51, slap her. Across the face.'

Erica could not help herself. 'What?' she exclaimed.

'You heard. Slap her.'

Erica hesitated. The woman looked blandly back at her, devoid of any emotion. 'You're taking too long, 51.'

Erica raised her hand, unsure of what to do.

'Stop, 51,' said the loudspeaker. Whatever games they were playing, Erica was grateful not to have had to carry it through.

'6, you show her,' said the voice from above. 'Slap her.'

Erica hardly had time to take in what had been said before the woman struck her hard on her left cheek. Her hand shot up to cover it as she cried out in pain.

'Again.'

6 pulled Erica's hand away from her face and slapped again, then returned her arms to her side as if nothing had happened.

'See how it's done, 51? Now slap her, unless you want more yourself?'

Erica did not want more. She wanted to scream out, 'Haven't you hurt me enough?' But she knew her words would be wasted.

The woman stood waiting, looking into Erica's eyes. Almost imperceptibly she nodded. 'Do it,' she whispered. 'Do it, there's no way you can't do it.'

So Erica slapped her, the noise echoing round the room. 6's head jerked to the side and she yelped, making the blow appear harder than it had been.

'That fools no one, 6,' said the male voice. 'You'll be punished for that later.'

'Sorry, Master,' she said.

'Silence, 6. Stay still. 51, slap her again. And make it hard unless you want another public flogging.'

Erica did her best to turn off her emotions. She reached out and slapped, hard, turning the woman's cheek white, then red.

'Again.'

Erica slapped again.

'The other cheek. Backhand.'

When she had struck she knew that one had hurt, bringing a tear to the woman's eyes.

'Again.'

Erica slapped again.

'6, slap 51.'

Again the older woman's movement was fast and accurate. Erica was well aware what the mystery man was after - getting them angry so they would strike out in revenge. She wondered how many times her opposite number had been through this and how many times in her uncertain future she would have to.

'Again.'

Erica kept her arms by her side as 6 struck. She resolved not to cry.

'Backhand.'

The blow sent her spinning, almost knocking her over, but she turned her face again to await whatever was next.

'Stop now. Discuss this.' The speaker went silent.

'I'm sorry I hurt you,' 6 told her.

'Me too,' Erica replied. 'Was that to make us angry, so we'd fight?'

'Possibly. Possibly just to show us how to obey. I've learned to do that. There's no way you can win. Fighting them just gets you more pain and humiliation. Obedience is better.'

'Just how far would you go to obey them?' Erica wanted to know.

'As far as they told me to,' came the simple reply.

'What if they'd told you to really harm me?'

'Then I would.' She paused. 'I've nothing against you, 51. It's just survival, that's all that matters.'

'And if they ordered you to remain still while I really harmed you?' Erica asked quietly.

'I'd fight. Like I said, it's survival.'

'I just want to cry.'

The blonde took up the kneeling position quickly.

'What is it, 6?' came the male voice.

'May I comfort her, Sir?'

'You may.'

She rose and put her arm around Erica's shoulder, encouraging her to lean into her and cry. Erica allowed all the emotion to flow from her until her tears ran onto the woman's breasts to be soaked up by the bra she wore. The blonde made comforting noises as if she were cuddling a child. 'All right now?' she asked.

Erica nodded and sniffed. She even managed a smile.

'I'll get you some tissues.'

Erica watched the blonde go to the bathroom and press the button. The door swung open for her to enter. Moments later she brought tissues back to hand to Erica.

'51, stand,' the voice said again.

Erica wanted to shout back, to fight, to say, 'Leave us alone!' But she knew it would be futile. She was too weak and too hurt to resist, so she stood.

'6, kneel.'

The blonde dropped to her knees in front of Erica.

'Instruct her, 6,' the voice said. 'Tell her she must obey, no matter what.'

'Yes, Master,' the kneeling woman said dutifully. She looked up at Erica, softness in her eyes. 'Just obey them, 51. It's stupid to fight. You're too weak. Just do what they say.'

Erica nodded.

'Well, 51?' questioned the speaker.

'Yes, Master,' she conceded.

'Are you going to do as instructed?'

'Yes, Master.'

'Good, 51. Now, without hesitation, slap 6 as you were told before.'

Erica did not dare think. Erica struck out.

'Again.'

She slapped again.

'Harder.'

She slapped harder.

'Again, harder.'

The blonde looked up and nodded. Erica slapped her again. She fell sideways from the force of the blow.

'Stand, 6,' the voice commanded. '51, take off her underwear. Do it now.'

Erica moved to the blonde, avoiding her eyes as she unhooked the bra and slipped it down her arms, dropping it on the bed before sliding the thong down her legs and off.

'Lean over the foot of the bed, 6,' the voice told her. '51, go to the second drawer, you'll find a number of riding crops. Select one.'

As the blonde moved to the bed Erica chose a crop. She had no knowledge of what was severe and what was gentle, so she picked at random.

'Stand behind her, 51.'

'Yes, Master.' Erica knew this scenario. She had already been on the receiving end.

'Six on each buttock, 51. If I even suspect you are being lenient you'll keep going until I'm satisfied. However many over and above six I have to allocate, 6 will do back to you. And I can assure you 6 won't be in the least bit lenient.'

Erica heard other male voices chuckling before the microphone was clicked off.

'Just do it,' the woman said. 'You can't afford to be soft, believe me.'

'Silence 6!'

'Sorry, Master.'

'Proceed, 51.'

Erica knew she had no choice. And her conscience had been beaten out of her. If she did not whip 6 hard enough the treatment would go on longer and she would suffer more herself. She could not even think of suffering more herself. It was that selfishness borne of self-preservation that made her lash the crop across the woman's buttocks until she screamed and cried, and to her shame Erica realised she had not even kept count.

'Stop now, 51,' the speaker called. 'We said twelve and you've delivered fifteen already.'

Erica threw down the crop in disgust and went to check on her sobbing friend, who turned to face her, their arms slipping around each other in comfort. Erica's thoughts were no longer her own. She had inflicted terrible punishment on this woman without any regret at all and now, driven on by some kind of warm passion she could not even begin to understand, their bodies were pressed together, wanting contact. Erica turned her face to 6 as, by some mutual sixth sense, the two melded into an open-mouthed kiss, with Erica giving just as good as she got.

The woman's arms were around her waist, pulling her in, uncaring about the stinging in her bottom as she sat on the bed, pulling Erica on top of her, their lust for each other overtaking all external sensations, yet each knowing their surrender to their own debauchery was being watched by the observers on the camera.

Uncaring, Erica slid willingly downwards, repeating what she had learned with Emily, wanting to give this woman pleasure after the pain and unsure whether there was a difference. The men had driven her to this and she bitterly hoped they enjoyed the spectacle.

But even that was to be denied her. 'Stand, both of you.'

Erica sighed. So did 6. They stood, breathing hard, coated in slick perspiration.

'Time to leave, 6. 51 needs her rest, needs her strength back. She's to be marked on Friday.'

'Oh God,' Erica cried.

'Yes, Master,' the blonde said, picking up her bra from the bed and moving to get her thong.

'Leave those. Leave everything. Just go.'

The door swung open. 6 dropped the clothes where she stood and walked out of the door without a glance back. The door closed behind her, shutting the world away once more.

'You did well, 51,' said the same gruff voice. 'Now eat, and then get some rest.'

CHAPTER 6

They left Erica alone for the rest of the day, apart from regular attention from the doctor and the nurse and more visits by the first girl she'd met, 36, to bring her food and refreshments. Despite the nagging terror of the ritual awaiting her she ate hungrily, as if she'd not been fed for days. 36 surprised her by pressing a switch on the wall, opening a small panel to reveal a television set. She was allowed to explain the controls, giving Erica a choice of piped video programmes and films. There were no programmes broadcasting dates, times or news, reinforcing the girls' removal from normal society. Erica half-heartedly watched a movie, but struggled to concentrate on it.

The doctor gave her a sedative injection before she was settled down for the night.

The next morning brought more of the same attention, and a long soak in the bath helped relieve some of her discomfort. The loudspeakers stayed silent throughout.

After she'd had breakfast a man she had not seen before came to the room. He was in his forties, she guessed, small in height yet very muscular and self-assured. His ginger hair was well-groomed and that, combined with a black suit, white shirt and blue necktie, made him look more like a respectable businessman than a cruel gaoler. He placed the small case he was carrying on the bed before flicking open the catches.

'I'm Don,' he started. 'We thought it's about time we saw you dressed. Put these on,' he said, handing her the expected thong, bra and suspender belt, all in white.

He sat on the bed to watch as Erica fitted the suspender belt round her waist and fastened the two hooks and eyes behind her. The label was still attached by its plastic tag. She tried to break it, but could not, so he beckoned her close, the smell of his cologne drifting up to her nostrils as he pulled the thong to one side and broke the tab. He indicated she was to continue dressing, telling her to hand him the other clothes to remove the tags. She held the thong as she stepped into it, pulling it to her waist and arranging the suspenders inside the legs. As she fitted the tiny bra the man opened the pack of stockings. All the items fitted her perfectly. Whoever these people were knew all there was to know about her. Maybe they measured her when she was first kidnapped, or maybe they got her sizes from her old clothes, wherever they were now. Destroyed, probably, like the rest of her past.

He watched avidly as she rolled the stockings up her legs. She had only ever worn stockings a few times, always in an outrageous, provocative way to shock the viewer. She had never worn anything like these non-stretch nylon ones and was not at all sure how to handle the seams. Don twirled a finger, ordering her to turn her back, and fiddled until both seams were straight and the suspenders tautly fastened. He opened a shoebox and passed her the high-heeled stilettos, another new experience for her. Once she put them on he had her walk up and down while he coached her how to walk elegantly in them. Erica felt about a foot too tall.

When he was happy with her deportment he surprised her by taking a dress out of the case, telling her to put it on. She moved across to him to take the dress and was immediately impressed by the feel of it. Black velvet encrusted with gems at the neck and around a diamond-shaped vent above the bust. She unzipped it and stepped in, pulling it up over her hips and sliding her arms into the short sleeves. Don stood and zipped it up. It fitted like a second skin, hugging her figure and moulding round her breasts and bottom. The hem fell to her ankles, but a slit up the front, again lined with jewels, reached to crotch level.

'Walk up and down,' he told her, sitting on the bed again.

As she obeyed the slit parted, showing the whole of each leg up to the tops of her stockings, and she had little doubt it would show even more when she sat down.

'Very elegant,' he told her. 'You may thank me.'

Erica turned to face him. 'Thank you, Master,' she said.

He laughed, shaking his head. 'You're new here, aren't you? That wasn't quite what I meant. Come here.'

Erica walked over to stand in front of him. He reached up slowly, taking his time, running his hands over her body, assessing her curves through the dress. She wanted to react, to push his hands away, to be her own self. Yet she knew it was impossible; he had the power to let her be safe or to endure terrible punishment, and she'd had enough punishment. At least his hands were gentle. He reached for the slit in the dress, exploring her, travelling upwards to the front of her thong and then down, between, making her squirm in a mixture of wanting it to stop and wanting more.

'Stand still,' he told her as he rose from the bed. He quickly and tidily undressed, folding his clothes over the back of the bedside chair, not casting a glance her way until he turned, naked, to face her again. She had been right about his physique; there was not an ounce of fat on him, so it was clear he kept himself fit. She could not help noticing he was half erect and was not sure whether to be insulted that he wasn't more so after his attentions to her body. He sat on the bed again, swinging his legs up and settling back until he was leaning against the headboard.

'Come here,' he beckoned, patting the mattress beside him.

Once again Erica knew this was no time to fight. She fully intended to tell the courts about it all when she eventually escaped, along with all the other abuses she was keeping careful mental notes of. They would regret this, all of them, when she got to tell her story. But for now she would have to go along with everything. No point in encouraging more punishment, so she joined him on the bed, the slit in her dress opening wide as she did so.

'Suck me fully erect,' he told her bluntly.

Dutifully she bent over him and opened her mouth wide to take him inside, while he lifted her hair to the side so he could watch. In his semi-erect state she could take most of him into her mouth, but gradually he swelled until she had to back off, moving her head slowly up and down his shaft, feeling him spasm every now and again as she sucked extra deep.

'Good, good,' he encouraged.

She set about a steady, deep rhythm. She assumed he wanted to come in her mouth and decided she may as well do her utmost to get it over with as soon as possible. As her head rose and fell faster and faster the links in her collar provided the percussion, clinking each time she bobbed.

But Don had no intention of coming in her mouth. 'Stop now,' he told her. 'Climb over me. Kneel.'

Erica sighed and raised herself above him, the slit opening wide enough for her to straddle his legs, showing all of her stockings and suspenders and most of the thong.

'Pull it aside and slide down over my cock,' he said, his voice deeper than before.

Erica reached down and pulled the thin strip of material covering her pussy to one side, then raised herself up over him, steadying his cock with her hand until she felt it at her entrance, then sinking slowly. She always enjoyed the very first moment of penetration whenever she had sex, and her body did not let her get away with it this time, making her moan out with the beautiful, searing feeling of surrender it brought. She desperately wanted to dislike it, but despite herself it felt good to be filled, partly because this felt normal. There were no bonds, no whips, no pain, no other women, just raw sex between a man and her. Granted she did not know Don, just his name, but that had happened before in her life. She closed her eyes and tried to imagine she was on a beach somewhere, under the warm sun, screwing with a faceless lover, with no walls to stop the daylight and the breeze and the sounds of a normal world reaching her.

She rose and pressed down slowly, feeling him slide deep within her, feeling his hands on her hips, pulling her back onto him before she went too far away. She felt him push his hips off the bed to stay within her and she felt the liquid warmth that joined them. Cutting through it all, insistently taking her created images of freedom from her, the metal collar around her throat, its weight and its annoying jangling forcing her back to her reality. She opened her eyes.

He had stopped moving, content to lie back and let her do the work, watching her rise and fall over him, a prisoner to her own lust.

'Do you like the dress?' he smiled up at her.

She nodded.

'Speak.'

'Yes, Master,' she breathed, unable to stop her rhythmic rise and fall and the contractions of her inner muscles around his shaft.

'It suits you,' he continued. 'Have you any idea how much it cost?'

'No, Master.'

'Just over five thousand, plus a few hundred to have it altered to fit you so perfectly.'

Five thousand pounds! She would never pay anything like that for a dress; the most she had ever paid was three hundred, and that was for her best friend's wedding. And here she was being screwed in a five thousand pound dress! 'What if it gets ruined?' she had to ask. It seemed such a waste. What could be the point?

'That's not for you to worry about. Silence now.'

He thrust hard up inside her to emphasise his control, gripping her hips harder, forcing her up and down, faster and faster until he went suddenly rigid and erupted inside her. She wanted to remain detached and dispassionate, but feeling him ejaculate took her the last few steps over the precipice that was her own orgasm.

With it came feelings of cheapness. Erica hated herself. She needed warmth and human comfort at a time like this. She sat back on him, feeling the last of his convulsions inside her. She placed her hands palm upward on her thighs and waited.

'Speak,' he breathed at last.

'May I kiss you, Master?' She hated herself for asking, but she needed some humanity.

He smiled up at her. 'Yes, you may.'

So she leaned forward, resting down on his chest as her lips sought his, kissing gently at first and then with more passion, using her tongue and lips and teeth, closing her eyes and trying to imagine herself free again. She was the one doing the kissing, not him. She was controlling the pace. And he, still within her, was growing again because of what she was doing, because she was turning him on. He was moving again, fully erect, thrusting into her, the wet sounds serving to amplify his lust for her. She ceased to care about the dress; let him worry about their mutual passion damaging or staining such a lovely piece of clothing.

Suddenly he moved, rolling her off him, pushing her to her hands and knees in the centre of the bed, parting her legs and kneeling between them as he rucked the dress above her waist. She rested on her elbows, waiting for him to be inside her again, impatient for her warm wet emptiness to be refilled. She felt his cock nudge against her buttocks as he gripped her, taking himself in hand to steady his aim.

His first thrust back inside her was hard and deep and was just as quickly gone. He had used it to lubricate himself. Next time his aim was higher, between the cheeks of her bottom.

'No, please!' she cried, suddenly realising his perverse intent.

'Silence!'

He pushed slowly, steadily and firmly, until he was buried deep in her anus. It immediately reminded her of Emily and the dreadful implements she had used there, yet it was different, more natural, more human.

He was gentle at first, sliding nearly all the way out and then all the way back inside her again, clearly getting off on how his large erection could possibly fit inside such a slim, perfect body. It was obvious a part of him wanted to possess, to demonstrate his ownership, to have her regardless of her wishes. He thrust harder, faster, delighting in her submissive moans.

Erica hated herself. She liked it. She did not want to, but her hips had their own agenda. They thrust back at him despite her mind telling them not to. She wanted him even deeper inside her rectum. She started to have powerful imaginings of how he would be so deep inside her she could feel him in her throat, and had a sudden vision of him coming in her mouth from within and his semen dripping down her chin as it escaped her. In this crazed state, overcome by lust, she did not care where his cock was now, she wanted it all, everywhere at once, filling her with its power, drowning her with its seed.

She put her hands down on the bed, wanting to ask the question, hoping he would notice.

'What?' he gasped. 'Speak.'

'Please, Master...' her voice jerked from his thrusts. 'Please come in my mouth.'

'That's my decision, bitch,' he growled. 'Silence.'

Her comments made him more urgent, more desperate to abuse her, to take all of her. But she had sown the seeds of a very erotic idea. She was the rebel he had seen flogged in the restaurant, the fighter Emily had told her of, the strong one he had watched on the video monitors. And here she was a victim to her own animal lust. Maybe letting her have her own way this once would make her more compliant. Maybe he would do it.

As he imagined pulling out of her rectum and shoving his cock in her mouth he felt his climax getting close, the point where his leg muscles tensed and his temples started to pulse. He was seconds away. As he felt his come start to rise up his shaft he pulled free of her, pushing her roughly on her side. Taking a handful of hair he pulled her head down.

Erica opened her mouth wide to receive him, almost gratefully accepting him into her throat. Immediately she felt him convulse. She concentrated hard, wanting to feel the moment his come sprayed into her. The first spurt hit the back of her throat, welling there until she swallowed. She backed her head off slightly until the head of his cock rested on her tongue and she could feel how the next few sprays burst forth. There was no taste, no smell. Somewhere from above he grunted and stared down at her. She did not want to swallow, not yet. She wanted him to see what he had done. What she had done.

She waited until he finished filling her mouth and pulled out, sinking back onto the bed beside her. She quickly adopted the position again.

'You want to say something?' he croaked wearily.

Erica shook her head. He looked puzzled until she settled down on the bed next to him and pointed to her mouth. As he watched she opened it slowly, letting him see the sticky whiteness on her tongue. A trickle escaped, running down her chin. She raised a finger to retrieve it, feeding it back between her glazed lips, and a very erotic idea came to him. 'Don't swallow,' he said. 'Keep it there until I say. Send in 21,' he called up to the camera.

'21 is rather tied up at the moment,' a female voice responded.

'How about 29?'

'She'll be there. Any requests?'

'Naked,' he told the speaker. 'Hands tied behind her.' He turned to Erica. 'Don't swallow now. Not yet.'

His words to the camera served to remind Erica that others had almost certainly observed her actions and her capitulation. The possibility that all this could be recorded had crossed her mind before. If it ever got out it would ruin her stepfather's political ambitions forever. But there was not much she could do about that now.

Don rose from the bed and made her stand too, just as a buzzer sounded at the door. 'Open,' he said.

Erica had noticed the girl who entered at the restaurant. She was the one who dropped a dish and was publicly spanked for it. Her dark hair was cut fairly short, and apart from her collar she was naked, even to the point that all her pubic area was shaved, making her look younger than she probably was.

'Come in, 29,' he said. The door closed behind her. 'Turn,' he told her.

29 slowly turned so he could see her arms and hands, securely bound together with several turns of white rope, one length holding her wrists and another above her elbows, pulling them tight together, causing her shoulders to arch and her breasts to thrust forward.

'This is 29,' he told Erica, somewhat unnecessarily. '29, you've already met 51.'

The two girls made eye contact but there was no verbal communication, merely a slight physical acknowledgement of one another.

'I've just come in her mouth,' he told the new girl before he spoke to Erica. 'Show her.'

He held her elbow to pull her forward to face the newcomer. 'Open your mouth, 51.'

The girl looked casually at Erica's lips as she parted them, then back to her eyes.

'Kiss her,' he told 29. 'Share it. And when you have I want to see. Only then may you swallow.'

The girl closed the space between them, offering her lips to Erica, her tongue immediately seeking hers with some enthusiasm.

'Did I tell you, 51, that 29 is a lesbian?' Don asked. 'She really doesn't like men very much at all.' He laughed as he watched them.

The girl seemed to know what to do, possibly because she had done it before. After all, a girl numbered 29 had to have been here for some time. She kissed well, her lips far more gentle than a man's as she sought out and withdrew the semen on Erica's tongue. When she was satisfied she broke the contact, leaving Erica rather breathless.

'Open,' said Don.

Each girl opened her mouth to show him what remained. When he was satisfied he told them to swallow.

'OK, 29, you can go now,' he said dismissively.

'Yes, Master,' the girl said as she turned to leave.

The familiar dull whirr of the door motors signalled its opening, but this time it did not close after the girl, and Erica watched her disappearing away down the passage, passing several other girls, some men and the occasional woman before going through a door in the distance.

'Right,' he suddenly said to her, 'time for a tour.'

Erica waited while he dressed, still aware of his residue in her mouth, and even more aware of the feel of 29's lips and tongue. Once he was fully clothed again he removed a leash from the drawer and attached it to her collar, more for its symbolism than to hold her with, since he applied no other restraints. His manner was one of a complete gentleman, yet he did not stand back to allow her through the door first, rather he led her. She felt like both a cherished lady and a worthless possession.

This time they did not turn right into the restaurant, keeping straight on instead until they reached the far end. Through the glass double doors facing them she could make out the waters of a large swimming pool, on the far side of which were floor-to-ceiling windows. As the automatic doors slid open the smell of chlorine took her back to her schooldays, to the swimming lessons she used to love.

Four girls and one man were in the pool, two girls swimming for exercise and the other two involved with the man. As far as Erica could see all were naked, the girls, for the moment at least, free of their usual collars. While the man fondled the breasts of one of them the other kept coming up for air before disappearing below the surface again, presumably to fellate him.

To the right of the pool another man was sitting in a jacuzzi, being served champagne by a costumed waitress while he watched two other girls performing an energetic *soixante-neuf* on the tiles in front of him.

Behind that, through full-height windows, was a large gymnasium, with a few girls on various keep fit machines, each in uncharacteristic leotards and trainers. Her escort explained that this was purely to act as support, to stop pulled muscles and so on. At all other times the girls had to wear the outfits given to them or wear nothing at all. Even in the gym, should a Master want it, any of the girls would have to remove the leotard without question.

Everything about her looked so strange and artificial, yet everyone there treated it as normal. Nobody paid undue attention to the fact she was so elegantly dressed yet was being led along by a leash.

'In any part of *The Complex*, if a Master or a Mistress wants you, he or she will have you. Any complaint or resistance on your part will be severely punished, either immediately or in public at some future time. You've already experienced public punishment and I don't imagine you want to again, do you?'

'No, Master.'

'You could well find someone will want more than one of you at once, or that several Masters will want to use you at the same time. Understand?'

'Yes, Master.'

He pulled her towards the jacuzzi, exchanging cordial pleasantries with the man there.

'Like these two, for example,' he continued, indicating the two girls still giving each other oral pleasure. Erica could make out the number 31 tattooed into a buttock of the top girl.

'They're here because this Master wants some visual amusement.'

'What's this one's number?' the second man asked, with a hint of a Scottish accent.

'51,' Don told him.

'Welcome to *The Complex*, 51,' he said, smiling.

Erica glanced at her escort, unsure whether this counted as permission to speak. He nodded slightly.

'Thank you, Master,' she said back.

'Polite, too,' the Scot commented.

'She is now,' Don said. 'She was trouble at first, but as they always do she succumbed to the initiation.'

'51, will you do something for me?' the Scot asked.

'Yes, Master.'

'Go and push your fingers inside... what's the top one's number?'

'31,' Don told him.

'Push your fingers in her.'

Don tugged the leash slightly in case she delayed. She squatted next to the two girls, the one underneath apparently glad of the break, resting her head on the tiles to allow Erica access to her partner. The upper girl's labia were soaked, so two fingers of Erica's right hand slid in easily.

'Put your whole hand in,' the Scot told her. 'Fist her.'

Erica blushed. She had never performed such an act, but with the Scot's guidance she squeezed her fingers together, making them into a tight conical shape and tucking her thumb inside them.

'Have you ever done this before, 51?' the Scot asked.

'No, Master.'

'Go steadily but firmly,' he instructed. 'You'll manage.'

41

So Erica pushed, sliding in easily up to the knuckle as the girl tensed and moaned.

'Push now, steady,' the man said.

The girl helped her, pushing back against her hand until it slid fully into the tight channel.

'Now explore her.'

To Erica it looked as though her forearm was growing out of the girl, whose pussy clamped her tight in its warm wetness. The girl moaned, her head arching back as Erica's hand twisted inside her. She tried opening and closing her fingers slightly.

'How does that feel, 31?' the Scot asked, moving to get a better view.

'Good, Master,' the girl breathed.

'Do you want her to make you come, 31?'

'As you please, Master.'

'Yes, as I please. But no, I don't please. You can wait. Take your hand out, 51.'

The girl's muscles seemed reluctant to release Erica, but eventually her hand slid free, slick and slippery from the girl's juices.

'Put your fingers in her mouth, 51.'

Erica did as instructed and waited patiently while the girl licked her own fluids from her hand.

'Well done, 51,' the Scot said, smiling appreciatively. 'I'll look forward to using you when you're ready. You two, carry on as you were,' he ordered as he settled back to his champagne.

Don pulled the leash again, leading her along the side of the pool to a small hallway fronted by glass doors. He did not stop, pushing the doors open to take her outside, the first genuine fresh air and daylight she had experienced since she'd been here. A grassy slope led upwards, with paved steps set into it. As they neared the top Erica got her first glimpse of how vast the grounds were. The land sloped very gradually away in front of them, to trees and shrubbery in the distance.

Over to the right stood wire netting fences enclosing five tennis courts, only two of which were being used by people in regular tennis kit, so probably not slaves. As she watched one of the girls, dressed as usual in heels, stockings, bra, thong and suspenders, came from a door near the restaurant with a tray of drinks and sandwiches, taking them to a table beside one of the courts.

'If you want to run,' Don interrupted Erica's thoughts, 'it's that way.' He pointed directly ahead into the distance. 'But I warn you, there are video cameras, trip fences, a very high wall with razor-barbed wire on top, some very nasty guards and some very hungry dogs. But if you still want to try then feel free to at any time; it does amuse some of the Masters.'

'May I ask a question?'

'Ask away. I may even answer.'

'Has nobody ever suspected this place exists?'

That amused him. 'Suspected? Anyone who's anyone *knows* it exists. That's what keeps it running. No matter what happens there's always someone who can sort it out, keep it out of the papers and so on. We can do anything we like here. Anything at all.'

To one side of *The Complex* was a large ornamental garden, where twenty or so of the guests sat sipping drinks, talking, reading papers or just taking the air.

Again they were being served by the scantily-uniformed girls, one of whom, for reasons not explained to Erica, was hanging by her tied arms from a stout pergola, her toes inches from the ground and her face a mixture of tension and tears. Erica assumed she had done something wrong and was being punished, or maybe they just wanted her that way for decoration. Whichever it was, nobody was even looking at her.

Quite a few watched Erica approach, though, possibly because her elegant gown stood out from what everyone else wore. One man stopped her and reached into the slit, roughly investigating her pussy with his fingers without saying a word, while Don used the opportunity to chat to two women at one of the tables, still holding her leash loosely in his hand. A few minutes later, either bored or finished, the man moved back into the building and their tour continued.

The car park at the front of *The Complex* looked like a luxury car show. Rolls Royces, Bentleys, Mercedes and a whole host of cars Erica could not even name shone in the sunlight. As they watched a blue Aston Martin appeared in the distance, making fast headway up the sweeping driveway before stopping at the main doors, where its occupants - a man and a striking blonde woman - got out, leaving one of the masked men to park the car. Erica's mind was working fast. If she could get the keys of one of these, that could be a way out.

'Don't even think it, 51.' Don was ahead of her thoughts. 'The drive to and from the car park has spikes that have to be lowered to get a car in or out. The two sets of main gates - two in case anyone tried to ram them - are protected by armed guards and there's a pit that has to be raised to get a car in or out.'

'Just because one of us could steal a car and try to escape?' she asked.

'Did I say you could speak?'

'No, Master. Sorry.'

'In answer to your question, no, it's not because of that. We have politicians and foreign heads of state here. If anyone should attempt an assassination, or perhaps the gutter press tried to get in...' he left the comment incomplete.

Erica sighed and sank to her knees on the grass, her hands upwards. Don pulled her upright with the leash. 'Speak.'

'So people do know about this place?'

'Don't get your hopes up, 51. The only people who know about it will not be talking about it. If the press find it, it'll be because they manage to follow someone.' He held the leash in his left hand while he reached into his right pocket. 'Enough questions now. Open your mouth.'

The ball tasted of rubber and forced her mouth wider than was comfortable. The straps behind her neck held it firmly. When he had fastened the gag in place he used a cord to tie her hands behind her for the rest of the tour.

She was shown the medical facilities, a guest room, a small cinema, a full office suite where the guests could use secretarial services, photocopiers, faxes and phones.

Don went overboard in showing her how secure everything was, especially anywhere that could be used to communicate with the outside world. It was not ever a case of hiding the facilities so much as showing her how futile any attempts to use them would be.

Erica made mental notes. They could not be faultless. There had to be a way.

The tour took in all three floors above ground and ended in the basement, which Don referred to as the dungeon. It was fitted out with some extensive, evil-looking equipment, upon which two girls were bound.

One was on some kind of rack, her hands and legs being stretched by a woman using a remote control. The second was strapped to a cross, being whipped by the silver-haired man who had been in charge of her initiation. Erica was glad she was unable to speak, lest she fall foul of some rule and end up on one of these contraptions.

Finally she was taken to the restaurant, where the gag was removed and she was untied while Don enjoyed some coffee and sandwiches, served by another girl whom she recognised from her initiation.

'Do you remember her?' he asked.

'Yes, Master, from the other night.'

'She whipped you.'

Erica stayed silent.

'Would you like to get revenge for that?'

'No, Master, she was only doing what she was told.'

'You'll whip her anyway. Come here,' he called to the girl, 'and bring a crop.'

The girl hurried to a cupboard, collecting a riding crop and offering it to Don.

'Bend over that chair,' he told her, and she obeyed immediately. 'A question, 51?'

'Yes, Master. Why must I hit her? I don't blame her for what she did.'

'You'll do it for no other reason than I tell you to. I'm not concerned with your anger or blame. You could be desperate to whip her, but if I don't want you to it doesn't happen. But I do want you to, so you will do it.'

Erica stood, taken aback by his sudden anger. She mechanically raised the crop and then swept it down against the girl's bottom, not knowing whether she was doing it too hard or too soft, nor whether the girl's yelps and tears were real or for effect. By the time he let her rise her poor bottom was striped, blotchy and red, but strangely Erica felt no guilt at all. She had no control over events, and she knew that in the reverse situation the girl would have shown no mercy either. She was being turned into a heartless machine.

'Did you enjoy whipping her?' Don asked her.

'No, Master,' she told him honestly.

'Did you enjoy being whipped?' he asked the tearful girl. 'Speak honestly.'

'No, Master,' she echoed Erica.

'Good,' he smiled. 'If you liked it, it wouldn't be as exciting.'

Erica stored this information, thinking about it later, after she'd been retied and led back to her room, where she sat, helpless to do anything except watch the screen on her wall, showing a camera overlooking the garden terraces she had been in earlier.

The girl was still suspended from the pergola, still being ignored by the guests. She watched as another undressed in front of two couples before she carried on serving them their refreshments.

She knelt on the floor for attention.

'Yes, 51?' a female voice asked.

'Please, I need to use the toilet.'

Immediately the bathroom door clicked and swung open.

'With my hands tied?' she asked.

'Wait,' the voice told her.

A few minutes later 36, the first one she had met, arrived in her room.

'She needs the toilet, 36. Help her.'

Erica turned her back, offering her hands to be untied.

'Leave her tied,' the woman's voice said.

36 stood aside to let Erica enter the bathroom, blushing at the thought of what was to happen, sure in the knowledge this was yet another attempt to humiliate and thereby subjugate. She turned as she reached the toilet, waiting while 36 pulled up the dress and pulled down the thong before she sat down.

The girl waited, even managing a reassuring smile, perhaps aware the camera would not be watching her face. When Erica had finished the girl unrolled some toilet paper and wiped her dry.

'Bring her off, 36,' the woman's voice interrupted. 'Make her come.'

Maybe 36 had been here long enough to just accept such orders. Certainly she showed no signs of embarrassment as she pulled the thong off and pressed her fingers to Erica's pussy, seeking out her clitoris and circling it gently, making Erica squirm from the pleasurable sensations. She knew exactly what to do to quickly make Erica gasp and moan. The fingers became more insistent, until Erica's legs trembled and her mouth opened in a searing gasp, her hips responding, trying to make her own rhythm, trying to maintain that glorious contact.

Within moments she was there, reaching her peak, eyes closed, sighing, 'No, no, no,' regardless of the possible consequences of speaking.

When she recovered she caught sight of herself in the mirror, her hair a mess, her face a betrayal of the fact that once more her body had succumbed to a place her mind did not want to go. Post-orgasm, she resented the girl's fingers still within her, wanted to shout out loud and fight.

But nobody had told 36 to stop.

Nobody had told Erica to stop.

As she stared at her reflection she saw herself jerk, she watched her eyes glaze over again as the kneeling girl's practised fingers took her back up the slope to the inevitable conclusion, with who-knew how many unseen eyes witnessing her degradation. But this time they waited until the perfect moment, when Erica was about to crash over into orgasmic oblivion once more.

'Stop,' said a male voice.

36 stopped and removed her hand, but Erica could not. Jerking her hips forward, trying to reach for something that was no longer there, she orgasmed, taken there by her mind alone, dizzily sliding from the toilet to the beige carpet. She convulsed as 36 looked down at her. Erica wanted to stay there, to sleep, to close her eyes and dream she was free.

'Leave now, 36,' said the voice.

In the control room near the front door, a place none of the girls had ever seen, those who witnessed Erica's spontaneous orgasms watched her on the big monitor, listening to her sobs, excited by the display of stockings and legs and bound hands. Don was already formulating an idea as Erica drifted off to sleep where she lay on the carpet, and by the time her breathing slowed and regulated he had started discussing the details with the others.

CHAPTER 7

Erica awoke because of her arms. She had no feeling in the left one at all, so it was a struggle to sit up. Rolling to a kneeling position she managed to get to her feet, sitting on the toilet while she flexed her hands until the feeling returned. She glanced up at the camera, expecting some orders or comments, but all remained quiet. Maybe they had got bored and were not even watching. She decided to sit a while longer and have some peace.

Her face looked a mess, streaked with perspiration, her hair awry. The slit in the dress had fallen open, revealing the whole of her stockinged legs, but she did not bother to attempt to cover herself. It would probably amuse them and they had seen all there was to see anyway.

She stood and looked at everything in the bathroom - the bottles of shampoos and cosmetics, the hair dryer, the electric toothbrush, the mirror, the shower; not because she was curious, but it was something to do. She gave a few half-hearted tugs at her bonds, but they stayed fast. Erica was bored. She had no choices as such, nothing to occupy her, but found herself wondering whether this was some additional torture. Maybe they were trying to subdue her by showing her that even their mistreatment of her mind and body was better than solitary confinement. Maybe it was. Erica's edges were fraying.

Would staying there show defiance and strength, or were they just not watching? Was she so insignificant in their eyes that they did not even bother to watch her all the time? Would asking to be let out be a further sign of submission? She sighed. She had no answers, but she could not take much more of being shut up, so she sank to her knees, lowered her head and waited.

'Stay like that, 51, we're busy at the moment,' said a woman's voice. So they were watching, and a few minutes later the door clicked open to admit 36 again.

'We can talk,' she said. 'We have to shower.'

'Together?' Erica asked.

'Yes.' 36 untied the ropes and then helped her off with the dress, going back into the bedroom to place it carefully on the bed.

'Do you believe that dress is worth five thousand pounds?' Erica asked when she returned.

'It doesn't surprise me,' the girl answered. 'They want to show you that money is no object.'

Erica unfastened her bra and removed the shoes, stockings and suspenders while the blonde undressed quickly and turned on the shower. When the temperature was right she stepped in, telling Erica to follow. The cubicle was easily big enough for two but Erica wondered why they had to shower together, although 36's touch as she soaped and washed Erica's back was pleasant enough. She did not even mind when 36 turned her around and washed her front, paying as much attention to her breasts and pubis as everywhere else. If their aim was to make the girls more sexually alert or embarrassed, they failed, since their sexuality had become matter-of-fact. The girls had become objects. Maybe that was their aim.

'Will you wash me now?' 36 asked, handing Erica the soap.

With gentle curiosity Erica smoothed her hands over the other girl's skin, at first avoiding contact with anywhere that might be considered sexual. The blonde's reaction was to close her eyes and enjoy, and was so delightfully innocent that Erica forgot her shyness and just touched everywhere, including her breasts and her pussy, enjoying the feeling of actually connecting with another person without the cruelty of this dreadful place. 'You like this?' she asked.

'Mmmm,' came the other's confirmation. 'It's nice to be treated gently.'

That gave Erica the encouragement to show how gentle she could be, smoothing her hands over the wet flesh and washing some of the pain and horror away.

She did not pull back when 36 kissed her, finding it a welcome difference from the previous time, and soon she was kissing back, the soap falling to the shower tray, forgotten as the two young women crushed together in a passionate embrace, the invigorating water cascading over them as they kissed, their arms around each other as much for sympathetic comfort as for anything sexual.

'Are we allowed to do this?' Erica whispered, breaking away from the kiss.

'They'll soon let us know if we're not,' 36 told her.

Erica kissed her way down to the girl's breasts, wanting her, the need to make her own decisions driving her on. After sucking and licking her nipples Erica kept going until she was kneeling, willingly searching out the cleft between her friend's legs, snaking her hand back up the wet body to hold her breasts as she sucked. 36's hands were busy too, seeking out Erica's breasts to cup and caress while she trembled under Erica's inexperienced oral attention.

Erica did not want anything for herself. She had been selfish most of her life, a taker, ruthlessly treading on anyone to get what she wanted. But this was different, an overwhelming need to give, to make another human being feel good. She extended her tongue to flick around 36's clitoris, teasing it until she felt the girl's legs start to give, then holding her up by putting one leg over her shoulder, angling her head so she could spear her tongue inside, rapidly bringing her friend to a shattering orgasm, freed as she was to mumble, 'Oh my God... oh my God...'

Afterwards Erica let her slide down the shower wall until both sat in the tray, the warm water still cascading over them as they sat and enjoyed the afterglow.

'Can I do the same for you now?' 36 asked.

'Do you want to?'

'Oh, yes.'

Later on they dried each other and went through to the bedroom. Erica knelt to examine the numbers etched into 36's buttocks while the girl stood still. 'Did it hurt?' she asked.

'Yes, a little,' the girl said matter-of-factly.

Erica did not want to have it done, but knew the inevitability of it, so she wanted to think she would be stoic, would bravely withstand the pain.

'What about afterwards? How long does it take to heal?'

'About a week.'

'I'm scared.'

The other girl turned and pulled her up, putting her arms around her while she sobbed.

'I don't want them to see me weak,' she said, glancing at the camera.

'It makes no difference, 51,' the blonde said. 'They want you broken and obedient, but they also like breaking you. They like it if you obey, they also like it if you don't, but believe me, obeying is considerably less painful.'

'I guess so,' she whispered.

'Time to get dressed,' the speaker told them. 'Not you, 36. You stay naked. 51, put the dress and some clean underwear on. 36, show her where everything is. She's to be dressed as before, but no bra this time.'

36 showed Erica the wardrobes, which slid open with expensive efficiency. They were lined with clothes, from the elegant to the tarty, including various uniforms.

Behind the leftmost door stood a multi-drawer unit, full of enticing lacy underwear. A drawer of thongs and knickers, one of bras, one of suspenders and stockings and one of slips. The lower drawers were dedicated to rubber and leather. To the right a cabinet contained dozens of shoes and boots.

As Erica gazed at it all 36 took out what she needed; a black underwear set and a new pair of seamed stockings. Erica dressed herself this time, checking with 36 that her seams were straight and finally asking her new friend to zip her into the dress, her breasts firm despite the lack of a bra.

'36, fit her with the chains.'

The girl obeyed instantly each time the voice spoke. From the bottom drawer of the unit she took out one of the chain contraptions Erica had seen various girls wearing, clipping the chains to her collar before fastening the cuffs around her wrists and ankles. When fitted it hardly restricted her movements at all.

'What's the idea of these?' she asked. 'They don't exactly impede me.'

'They're more symbolic really, like part of the uniform, but the Masters can clip them together if they want, or attach us to something with them. All ready?'

Erica looked at herself in the mirror. She saw a young woman she hardly recognised, tall in her heels, elegant and feminine in the superb dress, sexy in the slinky underwear.

'What are they going to do to me now?' she asked.

'No idea,' the blonde replied. 'And even if I had they'd probably stop me telling you.' She paused a few seconds, watching Erica look at her reflection. '51?'

'Yes?'

'I just want to tell you, when I have to whip you and stuff... there's no hard feelings.'

'I know,' Erica assured her. 'Same here.'

'We have to do it properly or we just get more ourselves, OK?'

'OK.'

'Silence now,' warned the voice.

The two sat on the bed, waiting anxiously for the door to open. When it did Emily was there accompanied by two of the masked men. She looked so different this time. Gone was the severe suit, replaced instead by a short flared dress in deep-blue satin.

Emily looked at the blonde briefly. '36, go to the restaurant.'

'Naked, Mistress?' the girl asked.

'Did I tell you to dress?' Emily asked, one eyebrow raised.

'No, Mistress. Sorry, Mistress.' She glanced quickly back to Erica, and was gone.

'You look good, 51,' Emily told her.

'Thank you, Mistress,' Erica replied, cautious not to incur any wrath, anxious as to what was planned for her. She prayed it would not be another ritual beating like the last time.

'Bring her,' Emily barked at the two men, who each took an arm and marched her out of her room, following the swaying bottom and sexy legs of the woman in front.

They followed the same route as before, along the corridor and turning right to the busy restaurant, straight through the doors and towards the dreadful platform topped by the binding posts. Erica wanted to pull back and run, fearful of the same treatment, but the two men held her firm. A few heads turned to watch her as she passed, seemingly anticipating some treat she was unaware of.

They led her onto the stage again, quickly unfastening her chains so they could rope her hands to the tops of the posts before dragging her legs wide and tying her ankles to the bottom. Once again she stared helplessly out over the assembled diners. She saw her stepfather's friend James again, sitting talking to a man she recognised as a TV chat show host, whose public whiter-than-white image would be destroyed if people knew he was part of this place.

All around slaves served food and drinks, never giving Erica a second glance. Emily walked towards her and clicked on the microphone.

'Ladies and gentlemen, tonight we have something rather special for your entertainment,' she announced. 'We're not going to rush it though, so enjoy your meal.'

'Is she still a disobedient bitch?' a man's voice shouted from the left.

Emily smiled and moved next to Erica. 'What's your name, slave?' she said, pushing the microphone towards Erica.

'51, Mistress,' Erica responded.

'Are you a disobedient bitch, 51?'

'No, Mistress.'

Emily addressed the audience again. 'Notice 51's elegant gown, ladies and gentlemen,' she said. 'Do you know how much it cost, 51?'

'Five thousand pounds, Mistress.'

'Over five thousand pounds,' she corrected. 'You have been careful with such an expensive item, haven't you, 51?'

'I've tried to be, Mistress.'

'Good,' the woman said. 'Good.' She walked round behind Erica as she talked, and when she appeared again she was holding a frightening looking knife. She put the microphone down and stood in front of Erica, staring into her eyes. Lowering the knife she placed it inside the dress, at the top of the slit.

Erica heard the rip as she moved, feeling the air touch her stomach as the dress parted. A few more cuts with the knife and the front of the dress was split completely, leaving Erica's breasts bare and the almost see-through thong showing her pubic hair to the assembled diners. Emily walked behind her again, using one movement to shred the back of the dress, finally moving to her sides to slit the shoulders, letting it fall to the floor at her feet.

Erica was stunned. They had gone to great lengths to impose the value of the dress on her mind. She had thought it was to make sure she took great care of it and the message was that they would clothe her in the finest things if she behaved. Now she realised she'd had the message all wrong. The valuable dress was to show her just how rich and powerful these people were, so that ruining a five thousand pound dress for amusement meant nothing to them. Just as she meant nothing to them. They would destroy her just as easily and with as little conscience as they had destroyed the dress.

And worst of all, Emily could see the realisation on her face. Erica knew it. She could see it in the eyes of the smug woman.

'What's your name, slave?' she said into the microphone.

'51, Mistress,' Erica sobbed.

'And what value are you, 51?'

'Nothing, Mistress. Nothing at all.'

A ripple of spontaneous applause broke out in the room. They had beaten her. They had won. Erica sagged against her bonds, ready to crawl, ready to suck and fuck and do anything they demanded.

But nobody untied her. This had been an appetiser, nothing more. There were other things in store before they were through. A short while later 36 was told to bring her water and talk to her quietly.

'They'll get a new girl soon,' she whispered. 'Then you won't be the new slave any more. Things will settle down, you see. Come on, don't cry.'

A few of the diners would occasionally mount the stage and look at her, or touch her, or spank her, or feel her breasts or bottom or pussy. The women were more catty than the men; they wanted her to be a worthless slut, as if her total degradation made them somehow superior. One twisted her nipples painfully, and then pulled her pubic hair until she cried out. She slapped Erica's face and called for clamps, fitting them tightly onto Erica's nipples before returning to her seat.

When the meals were finished and coffee served nobody left their seats. Those not facing the stage turned their chairs to see the floorshow, whatever it was going to be. Erica noticed a tripod being set up on the floor in front of the platform, not obscuring anyone's direct view but allowing a large video camera to be mounted on it. As it was connected up Erica noticed the large TV sets mounted on brackets high on the walls flicker into life. As she watched her pubic area came into clear, obscene close-up. Emily mounted the stage and spoke into the microphone.

'36, come here.' Within seconds the blonde was next to her.

'Ladies and gentlemen, the main event of the evening. We were watching the new slave 51 in her room earlier. We arranged for 36 to masturbate this slave, timing it carefully so she would stop before her orgasm. We were amazed to see that despite stopping the slut orgasmed anyway. As far as we could make out she was trying to fuck thin air. We thought you'd like to see it.'

Again the applause rang out, but this time accompanied by a few ribald shouts and whistles. Emily moved next to Erica.

'51, do you like being whipped?'

'No, Mistress.' That was an easy answer, though Erica dreaded having been asked.

'No, of course you don't. Well you have a chance to avoid being whipped this evening. All you have to do is to not orgasm. Understand?'

'Yes, Mistress.'

'Good. So that's the challenge, ladies and gentlemen. If she doesn't orgasm she doesn't get whipped.' Emily reached out and took hold of the thong and Erica yelped as she gave a quick tug, ripping it from her. As she unscrewed the clamps the blood rushed back into Erica's nipples and with it came the pain of feeling again. She cried out aloud.

Emily spoke again. '36, do you like being whipped?'

'No, Mistress.'

'Well, if you don't make 51 come you will be. Understand?'

'Yes, Mistress.' She lowered her head, dreading this.

'Your job won't be an easy one, 36,' Emily continued. 'But you did it once, earlier today, so you have to do it again now. When and if you make her come you must not be touching her pussy in any way when she does. And make sure you're not in the way of the cameras, so the Masters and Mistresses will be able to see every detail.'

Emily announced that bets could be placed on who would succeed. The blonde's naked breasts bobbled as she approached. At least the two understood each other. No mercy would be given, nor expected. Both girls would try to avoid a whipping. They understood each other.

36 moved around Erica, gyrating her body close so they touched with the faintest of caresses. Her hands wandered over Erica's breasts, down her stomach, along her cleft and deep inside. She attempted to bring her lips to Erica's, to renew the sensuality they had experienced in the shower, but Erica twisted her head away. 36 shrugged and concentrated on her breasts instead, her lips seeking the nipples, still red and sore after the clamps. Her fingers had already set up a rhythm, circling rather than touching, producing juices where Erica had been determined there would be none.

Erica concentrated on visions of her childhood, riding her horse through the meadows of the farm her grandmother owned in Wales. She closed her eyes and planned the route intricately, shutting out the invading fingers and lips. Each time she thought she was succeeding the bonds seemed to tug at her, pulling her back to the restaurant and the girl desperate to give her an orgasm. Her eyes snapped open, seeing the many eyes looking at her, willing her to lose.

She wondered if she had any champions in the room, whether anyone had bet on 36 losing. She suspected not. Maybe they knew just how good 36 was. Maybe they knew something about Erica herself she had never seen before.

As the eyes burrowed into her soul Erica already knew she had lost. She was their property, a worthless sex machine to be used and abused at the whim of other people. They had total control and Erica had none, she realised that now. And because she had no control she would not be able to stop her orgasm. They knew it. She knew it. And they knew she knew it.

36 was on her knees, her tongue starting Erica on her journey. She knew that an orgasm meant a whipping. So she would have to be whipped; nothing she could do. She could hear a young woman moaning, whimpering, gasping. She could hear herself. She could see her hips bucking in front of the hungry blonde head on six TV screens. She could feel the tongue vibrating on her clitoris. Her only chance was to come before 36 moved away. That was the deal, that's what she would do. She felt her legs trembling, knowing she was getting close, so she stopped resisting and let the feelings take over. Her only chance was to come as quickly as she could, to take 36 by surprise. Her pelvis ground forward. Her

hands clenched. She called out.

36 moved away a good two seconds before Erica reached her peak.

'No!' she screamed, watching her pelvis on the screen, reaching for the camera, wanting all eyes to penetrate her, to be inside her, the biggest gang-bang ever. Hardly a sound was heard from the diners as they watched Erica's pussy contract and pulse as she came, screaming out her defeat to the entire audience. Five, six times she tried to reach her non-existent lover, sobbing and gasping as her orgasm defeated her. To her side she saw 36's wry smile as she mouthed the word 'sorry' to her. She relaxed, unable to support herself any longer, sweat coating her body, leaving trails from her thighs and under her breasts and soaking into the suspender belt and stockings. Erica had no will for anything now. Only defeat.

The room came to life once the visual impact of what had happened had sunk in to the audience. One of the men who had set up the video camera stepped forward and pressed a few buttons before the recorded images came back to life, reminding Erica of her surrender. The girls who had taken the bets were moving around the hall again as Emily mounted the stage.

'36,' she said, 'you may return to your room. You did well.'

'Thank you, Mistress.'

Erica watched the naked girl walk towards the double doors, only to be stopped by a man and woman seated at a table next to the aisle. They said something to her, she nodded and the three left together.

'Ladies and gentlemen,' Emily announced again, 'we hope you enjoyed the performance. Anyone who bet on 51 has unfortunately lost. If those who bet on 36 will hand their slips to the slaves an order will be drawn up. The winners, in order, have the choice to go first or last.' She walked up to Erica and ran her hands over her back. 'You'll have to decide, ladies and gents, whether you want to mark skin that has not already been punished, or whether you'd prefer to add to the marks of others.'

Erica sobbed. OK, she knew she was to be punished and she had been so scared of it that the fear had found its level, leaving her unmoved, unthinking. But now they were to pile humiliation upon disgrace. They were already wandering to the front of the restaurant like they were queuing to settle their bills, each selecting what they would use on her, in the order of their estimates as to when she would climax.

Someone had turned up the sound on the screens so she could hear her own orgasmic cries echoing around the hall again and again. She heard someone suggest they video her punishment as well.

She sagged in her bonds as Emily pressed the remote control and the motors started to rotate her, turning her back and helpless buttocks to face her abusers. She closed her eyes as the first man stepped behind her and flexed his single-tailed whip.

CHAPTER 8

It took some time for Erica to recover. The doctor had tutted and complained how the second punishment had been done far too soon after the first, while Erica lay on her bed face down to meekly accept whatever lotions and dressings were put on her back, bottom and thighs. She was not bothered by any more punishments or sexual encounters; she was merely left to recover, locked into her room, spending unknown portions of days and nights watching the videos. She requested books, which were brought and given to her. She requested magazines that were refused. At regular intervals they brought food and refreshments, leaving her with a cordless bell-push in case she needed anything else.

The attention was so luxurious, so instant. Nothing was denied her apart from anything connected to her past or future. She could almost believe they realised they had made some terrible mistake and were making it up to her before they let her go. Almost.

36 visited often, the two being allowed to chat for long periods and the blonde applying relaxing massage, for which, she told Erica, she had been trained. Erica had no idea how long she was left like this, but she could not get around the restlessness. She assumed they would treat her the same as the others soon enough, making her available to the guests and requiring her to wait at the tables and serve drinks. At least that would mean she could use the library, the swimming pool and the gym instead of being locked into her four walls.

Gradually the wheals healed and the discomfort waned. She checked her back often in the mirrors, watching as the skin regained her original smooth colouring. She was lulled into a sense of boredom, of nothing happening. Visitors were regular and frequent, giving her a sense of day and night. Still she longed for a past that seemed so far away it could almost have been fictional. The more she tried to imagine her mother's face, the less she could remember the features.

When the soreness was at its worst she spent the day naked. There was no shyness any more, because there were no choices. The wardrobe doors remained locked and no clothes were supplied. The people who visited her did not appear to notice the fact that they were dressed and she was not, so it became the norm. The temperature of the room was kept constantly comfortable; so much so that she wondered whether that was another way of making time cease to matter. Just as darkness hid the borders between day and night, so a uniform temperature would hide the changing seasons. Only when they were allowed to go outside or into rooms with windows could they get a sense of time.

Then one day there was a change of mood. She could not tell why she felt it, but she did. She had the same number of visitors, from the other girls serving her food or sitting to watch videos, or even talking if it was permitted, to the regular visits from the nurse. The doctor had stopped calling by now, so she knew she was OK. The people who came acted much as they always had, yet Erica did sense a shift.

When Emily arrived accompanied by two masked men Erica knew something was afoot. They gave her a black thong to wear, and that was it. No bra, no shoes, no stockings. The men fitted the same thick leather cuffs she had been forced to wear on her first day, snapping the padlocks in place on each. Emily told her to sit on the bed.

'What's your name?' she asked.

'51,' Erica told her, weary of being shown her own weakness.

'Today that number will be your own for good,' Emily told her. 'Today you will be marked.'

Erica's stomach sank, feelings of nausea overtaking her. She looked up at the heartless woman who was quite clearly taking such sadistic pleasure in telling her. Erica dropped to her knees, crawling to her.

'Please, please, I'll do anything, please not that.'

'Silence, 51,' Emily growled. 'You will stay silent.'

Tears of terror fell down Erica's cheeks. She had known this moment would come and mentally prepared herself, but all that was bravado. Now she was faced with the reality she felt physically sick. She had to get out. She had to. The door was still open, so perhaps...

In a moment she was on her feet, springing towards it. Nobody reacted fast enough and she was through it. She ran, straight down the passage, heading for the entrance hall, knocking into another girl and sending her tray of drinks flying. The doors to the foyer were yards away and the shouting from behind her seemed a long way off. As she sprinted towards the daylight the doors in front slid quickly closed. She crashed into them, but they did not budge.

She could see two men running towards them through the small toughened-glass windows, so she turned, facing the way she had come, seeing the two masked men approaching. They had already reached the turning for the restaurant, so there was no way she could escape that way. All that was left were a few doors to her left and right. She tried the first but it was locked. The second opened and she crashed through, closing it behind her, looking for a way to lock it, to keep her pursuers at bay for a few more valuable seconds while she tried to find another way out.

Then she noticed them. The room was opulently furnished, much bigger than hers with a large four-poster bed in the centre. On it a fair-haired man was being attended by two of the girls, one sucking him deep, her head bobbing up and down while the other lay on the bed next to his avid eyes, masturbating with an enormous dildo. He looked up as Erica crashed in, while the two girls did not flinch.

'What are you doing here?' he shouted at her, but Erica was too busy looking towards the patio windows, already wide open to admit the fresh summer air.

The door burst open behind her as she dashed for the light. She almost made it, but before she reached the open air a hand grabbed her hair and yanked her back, throwing her to the floor, making her scream out. The two masked men hauled her to her feet, holding an arm each as Emily arrived in the room. She apologised to the fair-haired man, who dismissed her words, saying he had quite enjoyed some action for a change.

Emily faced Erica. 'Apologise to the Master,' she growled, but Erica stared back at her and remained silent. 'You never learn, do you?' Emily sighed. She nodded to the men, who quickly forced Erica to her knees. 'Now apologise!'

'S-sorry, Master,' Erica gasped, cringing with pain.

'Do you want to punish her?' Emily asked him.

'Yes,' he said casually, 'but not now. Is she the one to be marked today?'

'Yes. 51,' Emily told him.

'So,' the man continued. 'It'll take a few days to heal. I want to be the first to have her afterwards, OK?'

'OK, consider her booked.'

The men hauled Erica to her feet while the two girls remained faithful to their robotic tasks, as if none of this was happening.

'Where did you think you could go?' Emily sneered. 'Speak.'

'Anywhere,' Erica panted. 'Just away somewhere... anywhere.'

'But there's nothing out there, not for you. Nothing exists outside *The Complex*. But,' she tilted her head slightly as she continued, 'if you think you can escape, go ahead.' She spoke to the two men. 'Let her go.'

Immediately they released her arms. Erica looked at them, and then back at Emily.

'Go on, run!' the woman shouted, pointing at the open patio door. 'There's the way out.'

Erica did not move at first, certain that if she did she would be pulled down again. Slowly circling around Emily, watching her all the time, she backed to the opening, feeling behind her as she went. She backed slowly onto the small patio, glancing out of the corner of her eyes at the low parapet surrounding it and the lawns beyond. She took one last look at Emily before she ran, springing over the wall onto the neatly mown grass, sprinting away from the building as fast as she could.

A siren sounded behind her. Shouts joined the frightening noise and over to her left a large black 4x4 raced up the driveway, slamming to a halt to let three uniformed guards out. Erica veered left towards the trees, perhaps fifty yards away now, blood pounding in her head and breath rasping in her lungs.

She heard dogs barking just as she reached the undergrowth and trees, but she was too fired up to worry now. Onwards she ran, jumping over branches, fallen twigs hurting her feet. She ran on, sure in her step until suddenly her world turned upside down. Something had snared her foot and whatever it was tightened and whipped upward, taking her with it. She had no time to react and when she refocused the ground was swaying and something tight held her upside down by her right leg, her arms dangling helplessly towards the ground several feet below her.

Within seconds a dozen faces were looking at her, two fierce dogs barking and snarling. Then into the middle of the crowd strode Emily.

'You're lucky,' she said. 'There are many traps out here, and you find a mild one. Have you ever seen a gin trap?'

Erica did not answer, she just stared all the hatred she could muster back at her tormentor.

'Well, have you?' Emily snapped.

'No,' Erica spat.

'Cut her down and show her,' she told one of the uniformed guards.

The man moved behind the tree from which Erica dangled, taking a pocket knife from his jacket. A few seconds later Erica fell, crashing to the ground, slightly winded and grimacing at the sharp pain as she landed on her side. Another guard pulled her roughly to her feet.

'This way,' the first said.

They walked a few feet further into the bracken, in the direction Erica had been heading before the noose so devastatingly halted her flight. The guard searched for a few seconds until he found a broken branch, using it to gingerly clear away the leaves from a point he obviously knew well. The cold, black shape of a device Erica had only ever seen in books and films gradually came into view. A circle of sharp serrations pointed upwards, two metal bars across the centre.

'Imagine this was your foot, slave.' He grinned, though there was nothing pleasant about his appearance.

The guard holding her arm pushed her forward until she fell to her knees, her head pushed within inches of the device. The man put the end of the stick in the centre, and with a sudden jerk the circle snapped inwards and upwards, the jaws' interlocking teeth crashing together. Erica jerked back and screamed.

'That could have been your pretty leg,' Emily told her. 'Think of the pain of that. It would probably be broken now.'

A tear rolled down Erica's cheek.

'Let her go,' Emily told the guards. 'Now, 51, do you want to continue your amusingly futile dash for freedom or come back inside? There's about half a mile to go before you reach the perimeter fence, and the nearer you get the nastier our little surprises will be.' She paused. 'So which is it to be? Speak now.'

'I... I'll come back, Mistress,' Erica said sorrowfully, fully defeated.

'A wise choice, 51,' the woman said. 'Very wise. But just to make sure you remember this silly episode you can crawl back on your hands and knees.'

Erica's feelings bordered on claustrophobia. She was shut in, there truly was no chance of escape and the whole thing felt like it was closing in, crushing her under its enormous weight. But she crawled, as instructed, with Emily walking beside her while the guards and the dogs went back whence they came, their excitement over. Emily directed her to the left, round the side of the building, through the patio areas and past rooms where people looked out to witness her destruction, while all the time Emily walked beside her like an animal handler.

'Stand now,' Emily said as they reached the door near the tennis courts. 'I want you to show me just how obedient you can be. You are to be labelled today and there's no way to avoid that. You do realise that, don't you?'

'Yes, Mistress,' Erica whispered mournfully.

'Speak up.'

'Yes, Mistress.'

'So show me how you obey. Walk to the restaurant proudly. Keep your head up and walk ahead, up onto the stage. A man will be there to bind you to the frame. You can struggle or you can cooperate. I want you to cooperate. Will you?'

'Yes, Mistress,' Erica acquiesced. 'May I ask a question?'

'Ask.'

'Will it be you who does it?'

'The labelling? No, not me. The right to mark you has been the subject of an auction. The highest bidder wins. You may be interested to know you broke the record for the highest ever bid. That was because of your rebellious nature. They like that.'

Erica stayed silent. Emily was right. It was not avoidable. She had no choices, no freedom, no ability to resist. Emily had given her a chance to retain her dignity, so she would take it. 'I'll obey, Mistress,' she said as proudly as she could.

'Good, well done. I get really turned on seeing you trying to be proud like this.' She stood in front of Erica and touched her breasts. 'I can make life better for you if you make life good for me, Erica.'

That completely floored her. Emily had used her name.

'That is your name, isn't it? Erica?' Emily asked.

Erica was within a moment of falling into her trap. 'My name is 51, Mistress, unless you choose to call me something else.'

Emily smiled. 'Well done. I knew you'd learn. This way.'

She stood aside to let Erica walk inside, along the hallway and left towards the restaurant. Most tables were occupied with people drinking tea or coffee, with plates of sandwiches and cakes, giving Erica the impression that it was late afternoon. All eyes turned her way as she emerged through the swing doors.

Using as much elegance as she could muster, Erica walked down the aisle towards the stage, stepping up to where the silver-haired man who had presided over her first public whipping stood waiting. He smiled as she approached, moving aside so she could see the frame in the centre of the stage. The middle part was a padded bench, but to the sides and the back were stout tubular metal bars, clearly designed to hold arms and legs still.

Erica stood in front of the device, aware of the dozens of eyes watching her every move. She stood motionless, staring at the frame, and beside it was positioned a surgical trolley upon which were placed some utensils, which she guessed were tools for tattooing.

'Ready, 51?' Emily asked her.

Erica hesitated, but then nodded.

'Then go ahead.'

Erica looked back at her, noting the silence of the expectant crowd. She stepped forward, sinking to her knees and laying her torso along the padded bench, aligning her arms and legs with the cold metal bars, waiting to be strapped in. Emily attended to her legs, fitting links to her ankle cuffs and wrapping leather straps round her thighs. The silver-haired man fixed her wrists out in front of her before fitting more straps just above her elbows. Finally he pulled the two ends of a strap from each side of the bench, anchoring her waist firmly to the cool surface.

They wheeled another trolley in front of her, on top of which stood a television. Within moments it displayed her buttocks in sharp detail as, she assumed, the various other monitors around the room did. The tiny black strap of the thong hid almost nothing. Her buttocks, white and soft, awaited the inevitable pain of the tattooist's needle.

'Be brave, 51,' Emily told her. 'Anything to ask?'

'N-no, Mistress,' she stammered nervously.

'Open your mouth,' Emily told her, pushing a hard rubber bit-gag between her teeth before strapping it tightly in place behind her head. 'Bite on that. It'll help.'

Erica felt some comfort from being strapped so tightly. There was no chance now, no freedom to move or even speak. The inevitable had arrived and she just wanted it to be over with, so she could heal and get on with whatever life she was allowed to have. She let herself drift, not listening to the announcements being made in the hall. She did not care who had bid for her. Whoever it was did not deserve her attention, or hatred. Hatred would be wasted; she was sure they would find a way of turning it against her, so she decided that simple compliance was the only way to handle this ordeal.

A motor clicked in and the podium started to turn, relieving her of the sight of her buttocks, yet facing her with the sea of eyes watching and waiting. They were in no hurry for the climax - her pain - was also the end. They wanted to enjoy the spectacle for a while first, and Erica hoped her bland acceptance would take away some of their enjoyment. The podium turned slowly to let the audience watch her bound body and gagged face. The tension in the hall was electric; she could feel its power. Her moment was approaching.

A small commotion in the hall captured her attention, but she was not in the right position to see. Someone had arrived who had drawn the eyes of the audience. Erica waited to see who or what it was.

As she rotated further the newcomers came into view, and she could have wept with joy when she saw them! At the entrance doors, accompanied by men in uniforms, stood her parents. She wanted to call out, to accuse, to exact revenge on her torturers, but the gag stopped her. Her parents' eyes looked across the hall to her, and they broke from the crowd to stride forward to the stage as the rotation of the podium once again hid them from view.

'Ladies and gentlemen,' Emily's voice called from the speakers. 'The highest bidder, the one who gets to mark our newest slave, is our esteemed member... Laurence Pettinger MP!'

'Mmmm!' Erica screamed through her gag, shaking her head from side to side.

There had to be some terrible misunderstanding. 'Mmmm!'

'Don't be so shocked, 51,' Emily told her. 'Who do you think arranged for you to be brought here in the first place?'

The podium stopped with a jerk. From her viewpoint Erica saw the silver-haired man take one of the tools in his hand, making sure she could see the fearsome needle at its end.

'Master Laurence has elected to apply the second number,' Emily explained to the enrapt audience. 'The slave's mother will apply the first.'

Erica heard the buzz from the machine as her parents took their place behind her. Through her tears and screams she bit hard into the rubber gag, and waited.

CHAPTER 9

Erica wanted to sleep. She was dreaming of home, so long ago, when life was innocent and simple, when there was light and freedom and happiness. Why did they have to disturb her?

Time? What did time matter to her? There were no clocks here, no newspapers, television, radio or calendars. Erica had no way of assessing how long she had been a prisoner at *The Complex*, but she estimated about six months, based purely on the changing seasons which even the power that ran this place could not hide. Some slaves tried to count days, but as soon as the warders found any such count they put them in solitary confinement for a few days until they could be confident the count would be lost.

'51, time to get up. This is your final warning!'

The first time she had heard that order she ignored it and went back to sleep. The voice sounded so mechanical, so impersonal, that she believed it was automated. That was the one and only time she made that mistake.

Then, as she drifted back to her slumber, the door to her room opened quickly to admit one of the often leather-hooded guards and Emily. They took her quickly, dragging her from the bed and securing her arms to a ceiling hook in the centre of the room so tightly she had to stretch on tiptoe to keep some semblance of balance. There they whipped her, mercilessly and unheeding of her screams and her regrets.

Afterwards, as she hung loosely from the ropes with no strength left to support herself, she heard them leave. In the absolute silence that followed, punctuated only by her breathing and remnants of her sobs, she felt the trickle of sweat run down her back, stinging her welts as it meandered.

So Erica never ignored the wake-up calls again. She rose quickly, unashamed of her nakedness since she had no choice about it; the ever-watchful cameras had become part of the norm. Why worry about what she could not change? At least, that's what she wanted them to think.

Erica behaved herself, always. When she had first arrived at *The Complex* they broke her spirit completely. She was beaten and fucked, made to do any sexual act the Masters and Mistresses desired of her. Sometimes she recognised a politician, a media star or a sportsman. Occasionally the beast who wracked her body with pain was a squeaky clean pillar of society. She even numbered some of the nation's senior clergy among those who had abused her. In this place there were no laws other than those dictated by the people who ran it, whoever they were. The guests, away from the constraints of public life, took their pleasure from the girls, who were so depersonalised they were not even allowed names.

They were permitted leisure time, though, and but for their lack of freedom their surroundings were luxurious, the accommodation, facilities and catering of the standards of the very best hotels. They were denied nothing except any kind of freedom. Erica pondered how, during their leisure breaks, she had become firm friends with 21, a blonde about five years older than herself, and how once, in the grounds outside the main house, where they hoped the prying microphones could not hear, she introduced herself properly.

'Erica Pettinger,' she whispered.

21 looked at her blankly, then after a few seconds a tear welled in the corner of her eye, her mouth twitching as she started to cry.

'What's wrong?' Erica asked.

'I can't remember my real name,' the woman told her.

At the time Erica thought that hard to believe, but the longer she remained at *The Complex* the more she realised that the total lack of identity could easily brainwash her, and all self-respect, all self-esteem and even all sense of self could easily dissolve. So she resolved to remind herself of who she was every morning and every night, ready for the day she knew she would escape.

Erica Pettinger, daughter of... Laurence Pettinger, MP. Yes, that was it. Her traitorous, bastard stepfather. She well remembered that day when her parents had arrived at *The Complex* and she thought she was rescued, only to discover that they were the ones to cruelly tattoo her number into her flesh with a needle. 21 had advised her to forget the incident, but Erica wanted to remember. The memory continually fuelled the hatred she retained for her parents - her stepfather in particular. He would have been the main instigator of her misery, she was sure of that. *The Complex* had taken away her soul, so she knew she did not matter. She had nothing to live for and no prison could be worse than this, so when she did escape she was going to seek her revenge.

But that was for another day. Until she escaped she would obey. They did what they wanted to her anyway, so fighting them merely caused her more pain.

The camera watched her shower, then watched her dry herself and brush her long dark hair and apply her makeup. She waited for the bathroom door to be opened and walked back into her bedroom where, as usual, her clothes had been laid out on the bed by some unknown attendant. It was the same each day; get up, go to the bathroom, listen to the door lock, use the toilet, shower, wait for the door to unlock, after which her bed had been made and her clothes provided. Never once had she been permitted to see who did the work.

Today's outfit was all black. Black was by far the most popular choice. Erica looked under the dress to where a wispy suspender belt and a new pack of nylons lay. She shook the dress, not exactly surprised to find no other underwear. She sighed, thinking how immature people could be when they had absolute power.

She put the belt around her waist and fastened the two hooks and eyes, then opened the pack of stockings, smoothing them up her legs, checking the seams were straight before fastening the suspenders. She watched her reflection in the full-length mirrors as she stepped into the dress and smoothed it to her breasts before fastening the halter behind her neck, letting her hair fall back in place. Then, as usual, she sat on the end of her bed and waited for whatever might happen when the watchers clicked open the door.

After a few minutes the familiar clunk of the lock broke the silence and the heavy door swung silently open.

'You may go to the restaurant for breakfast, 51,' a woman's voice said over the speakers.

Erica stood and walked into the corridor. A workman stood aside to let her pass. She did not smile to him or speak to him. He was part of *The Complex* as far as Erica was concerned and if he had any human decency he would tell the police about the place and blow it wide apart. But he did not; he ignored what was going on, probably because he was well paid to ignore it. Maybe they let him use the girls from time to time. Whatever, he did not deserve any pleasantries from her.

21 appeared from her door as Erica approached and smiled when their eyes met. She wore a short dress with a flared skirt in deep-blue satin and teetered on high heels. They were not permitted to talk to one another in the corridors, but they had become adept at communicating with their eyes.

The two walked on until they came to the double doors that opened on a sensor as they neared. The large room was about half full, mainly with guests, though two other tables accommodated slaves like her. She had baulked at being called a slave at first, but the terrible reality was that she was one.

They had only walked a few paces into the room when a voice called from behind them. 'You two, stop there.' The voice was male and cultured, and a rugged face appeared in front of them. He was tall and athletic and Erica could not help thinking she had seen him somewhere before.

'Name?' he asked her.

'51, Master.'

'And you?'

'21, Master.'

'Take off the dress, 51,' he told Erica, stepping back a few paces to watch.

Erica did not hesitate, despite a slight buzz of interest in her predicament from some of those eating their meals. Around her a few of her fellow inmates served food and coffee, most glad that the focus of the guests' attentions was not on them. The halter sagged as Erica unclipped it, falling away from her breasts and stopping at the natural curve of her hips. She hooked her thumbs in the waistband and eased it off, draping it across the back of a vacant chair.

She stood, hands by her sides, as the unknown man looked her up and down. He twirled a finger round in front of him to signal for her to turn, which she did, slowly, feeling as if she were at some kind of market. When she had her back to him he moved closer, pulling her cheeks slightly to feel her firmness.

'When was the last time you were whipped, slave?' he wanted to know.

'Two days ago, Master,' she told him, remembering the occasion when her room had been visited in the middle of the night by a masked man and woman.

'For what reason?'

'I don't know, Master,' she told him honestly. 'Because they wanted to, I suppose.'

'Have you ever whipped anyone?' he asked 21.

'Yes, Master,' Erica's friend said.

'Ever whipped 51?'

'No, Master.'

'Has 51 ever whipped you?'

'No, Master.'

'It would amuse me to have one of you whip the other, but how shall I decide?'

Both girls assumed the question was rhetorical, or not for them to answer at least. Both were used to this, since quite a few of the guests derived perverse pleasure from watching the girls inflict pain on one another. They administered and received their beatings from each other without malice or feelings of vengeance. No mercy was expected nor given, since the penalties for showing any leniency were severe for both girls.

'I know,' the man said at last, 'get on the stage, and you,' he pointed at 21, 'strip as well.'

Without question Erica led the way, 21 followed, watched now by most of the diners. Frequently a guest would have an idea and put on a show for the others, and this was to be such a show. The two young women stood beside each other facing the assembled diners, watching the swarthy man. 21 looked nervous as she took her dress off and dropped it to the stage. Under it she wore a tiny white thong and a lacy white bra, through which Erica could see her nipples.

The man stood in front of the stage, watching. 'You, 51,' he directed, 'undress her fully. Do it slowly and give all my associates a show.'

Erica quickly moved behind her friend, reaching to unhook her bra.

'And at least look as if you mean it, 51!' The man's sarcastic tone shook her into action. She slipped both hands around 21 to cup the tiny bra to her breasts, and pressed her own naked breasts against 21's back, gyrating slowly in time with the soft music that filled the large room. Gradually she insinuated her left hand under the bra, cupping 21's generous breast and feeling the nipple rise under her palm. She dipped her head to kiss the woman's neck as 21 tilted her head to one side and closed her eyes. She too would go with the flow to avoid a beating.

Slowly, so as to provide a good show for the audience, Erica cupped the other breast too, allowing the bra to fall down 21's arms and drop to the floor, forgotten, her hands replacing the bra in providing cover for her naked breasts. She trapped both nipples between her fingers, bringing an involuntary gasp from the blonde.

Gradually she opened her fingers so the diners could see 21's engorged nipples poking through, turning her so she was leaning back, fully facing the audience. She moulded her breasts, still kissing her neck, bringing a moan of pleasure from her. Then she started to move her hand downward, slowly, teasingly, stopping now and again to make 21's skin tingle with expectation. Onward and downward once more, so that 21 held her breath and twisted her head round to be kissed.

Erica closed her eyes too. With their eyes shut they could almost believe they were free to do this, instead of performing because they had no choice. Their mouths opened, their tongues met and Erica's hand completed its journey, pushing under the waistband of the thong, down across the small springy curls of pubic hair to seek out warm wetness between the folds of the blonde's labia. She hooked her fingers into the oily recess, bringing a soft sob from her friend. The whole room, the whole *Complex*, did not matter at that moment.

But the euphoria did not last. Erica felt a sudden searing heat across her back and her eyes flew open. The crack of the bullwhip seemed to come a long time after the pain of its sting, though in reality they were one and the same. The man was standing there with a harsh grin on his face. He was already coiling the bullwhip up into his right hand, ready to strike again. In his left hand a second identical whip was already coiled.

'I said undress her, 51. Now do it!'

'Y-yes, Master!' she panicked.

Erica twisted 21 around to face her, quickly pulling the thong down to her feet, crouching as she did so. She hated doing this because the skin of her back felt taut and exposed, difficult for a man who liked to use a whip to resist. As she held the thong for 21 to step out of she sensed the man tense, but not soon enough for her to prepare for the whip's bite. The force of it knocked her over. The man was on the stage immediately, pushing her onto her back with his black leather shoe, the pain of the whip making her wince. The man beckoned 21 towards him, pushing her down until she was kneeling astride Erica's face and pushing until Erica's lips were smothered by her damp sex.

'Lick her, slave,' the man ordered, nudging Erica's arm with the toe of his shoe. Erica obeyed. She had become detached from the orders. In her mind she again turned the hatred she had for this latest in a long line of abusers towards her stepfather, and that made her lick with a vengeance, pushing her tongue up into her friend again and again as her eyes glazed over.

Before too long the man got bored and went back to his original plan. 'Stand, both of you,' he ordered, and when they were on their feet he circled them threateningly. 'How many strokes did I give you, 51?' he barked.

'Two, Master,' she said quietly.

'Louder!' he said, lashing across her bottom with the whip again.

'Three, Master!' she cried.

'Confused, are we, 51?' he taunted.

'No, Master. It was two and that made it three.' She could not disguise the defiance in her voice, and the man did not miss it either.

'Do I sense some rebellion in you, 51?' he mused.

'No, Master, I'm sorry.'

'Ask me for another and I might be lenient,' he offered.

Erica steeled herself. She had played out this scenario before. 'Please, Master, hit me again with your whip.'

She had hardly finished speaking when the next strike came, turning her legs to jelly with its ferocity. A loud scream escaped her lips, bringing a murmur of approval from the audience. If that was lenient, she did not want to know severe.

'How many is that now, 51?' he asked when 21 had helped her to straighten up.

'F-four, Master,' she sobbed.

'Good. Amazing how you can learn to count with the right encouragement.'

Erica hated the man. She hated all of them.

'Now, I suppose you're wondering why I got you up here.'

Both girls stayed silent, heads bowed.

'Well?' His voice was suddenly sharper, his hands tightening on the whips.

'Yes, Master,' they said quickly, as one voice.

'You're going to whip each other. And what's more, you're going to do it until one or other of you concedes. Any attempt to fake it will be punished in ways you don't even want to imagine. Whoever triumphs over the other will receive some special privileges. Understood?'

Both girls nodded nervously. The man handed them a whip each and moved them so they were facing each other. 'Ready?' he asked.

Erica tensed. 21 was her friend, but now she was also her opponent. She knew 21 would be too scared to go easy, and that she would not expect Erica to either. There would be no quarter given or expected, but this would not spoil their friendship. Besides that, the sooner this was over the better. They waited for the odious man to start the contest.

'Ah, but 51, you've had four strokes already and 21 has had none. That's hardly fair, is it?' he mocked. 'So you get the first four strikes, 51. And if you make them count perhaps you can defeat her without taking any more yourself. Worth a try, don't you think?'

'Y-yes, Master,' Erica said. And he was right; it was a chance of a reprieve. Erica's flesh was already smarting and if she could avoid any more then she would.

'Turn your back,' he told the blonde, and 21 gave Erica a nervous look as she obeyed. 'When you're ready, 51,' the man said as he moved away from the arc of the whip.

Erica let the coils of the terrible implement fall to the floor, holding the handle in her right hand. She moved into a position where she judged the whip would have the maximum effect, the tail of it lashing around with its inevitable crack and bite. Her hand tensed on the handle as she drew back.

Suddenly she brought her arm up and forward, as hard as she could, so that the tail would strike a vertical line midway between 21's shoulder blades. The blonde screamed as it struck, arching her back against the blow.

'Keep still, 21,' the man ordered. 'You'll get your turn, perhaps.' He turned to face Erica again, a sadistic grin playing on his lips. 'Harder, 51. Do it harder. Break her.'

Erica was not sure she could do it any harder, but she would give it a try. Drawing back she repeated the manoeuvre exactly, aiming for the deep pink welt that had risen down the length of 21's spine. The girl screamed again as she struck, falling to her knees and sobbing with the pain.

'Get up,' the man called to her, then turned to Erica. 'Help her up.'

Erica dropped the whip and moved quickly to her friend, putting her right arm round the girl's shoulder and helping her to stand again. 'I'm so sorry,' she whispered.

'I-I know, I would be too,' 21 stammered between sobs.

'Carry on, 51,' the man impatiently ordered.

The third blow followed the previous ones, making 21 squeal again, yet she did not sink to her knees this time. She stood, ready. She was determined to have her chance. Erica drew back one last time. She had to make this good. After the three she had already dealt if 21 got her chance for revenge it was going to hurt badly.

Summoning up all the strength she could she snaked the whip sideways, across her friend's tender back. The red weal arose immediately and moments later, when the worst of 21's shrieks had subsided and she once again sunk to her knees, Erica saw the livid streak of the strike, some six inches long in the centre of her back.

Yet within a few moments 21 was back on her feet, turning to face Erica. Her face was twisted, gasping from her ordeal, yet held a determination to succeed that frightened Erica.

The man was highly amused. 'Very impressive, both of you. I never thought you'd endure that, 21. But now it's all to play for. Last one standing wins. Wait until I tell you to start.'

The man stepped off the stage and pulled up a chair from one of the front tables. 'OK, you may begin,' he told them casually.

Erica tensed again, ready to reconvene the struggle, but 21 had already decided to act, lashing her whip out and catching Erica across her tummy, the end flicking round behind and nipping her bottom cheeks. She reacted immediately, catching 21 on her upper arm. It was a mistake, not having the damaging effect she hoped for. Worse still, the tip of her whip somehow became entangled round 21's bicep, so she could hold on and prevent further blows while she lashed out again and again at Erica, each blow making her yelp and making her weaker. Finally, with a supreme effort, Erica managed to pull her whip free, staggering back slightly right into the path of a high blow that caught her around her face, stinging her cheek and tangling in her sweat-dampened hair.

21 pulled, twisting Erica's head around with the whip, turning her back to face

her. As Erica put her hands up to try and untangle her hair 21 lunged forward to yank the whip from her hand and, transferring her own whip to her left hand, she pulled back to use Erica's against her.

From then on it was a lost cause. Countless strikes snaked across Erica's back and bottom and thighs until she was crying and screaming, weakening fast. And she knew she was losing. Even when she managed to get the tangled whip from her hair she no longer had the strength to fend off the assault. On her knees she turned towards 21, tears rolling down her face as she looked up, pleading for it to stop. 21 did stop, tossing the second whip away, out of Erica's reach and pulling her own whip back, ready to strike again. She was panting, coated in sweat, looking like a gladiator in the Roman arena, ready to kill.

The room had become tense with silence, the assembled audience sensing the end was close. The cruel man rose to his feet, taking a pace towards them.

'Stand up, 51,' he said quietly.

Erica sagged to her hands and knees, trying to gain some strength to stand. She got herself into a crouching position, and then slowly started to rise, wincing from the stinging fire permeating her body.

'What are you waiting for, 21?' he said. 'Finish her off.'

Erica knew she had lost. Slowly, deliberately, she turned her back on her friend, gritting her teeth for the final agony.

'Do it,' the man growled.

A second later the whip lashed across Erica's back, the stomach-churning retort cannoning around the room, accompanied immediately by Erica's weary scream. The audience watched as she seemed to hang there, held up by ever-weakening legs before slowly, slowly sinking to her knees once more.

'Do it again!' she heard from some seemingly distant point. The sounds of the room had become hollow and everything in it appeared to be moving away from her, as if she was falling, weightlessly, down some endless tunnel. The pain had blended into a state of mind she neither understood nor cared about. She closed her eyes and waited.

'Now!' the man demanded, and Erica felt the cruel lash burn into her back moments before everything flashed red behind her closed eyes and slowly faded to black.

Erica never saw or heard of 21 ever again.

CHAPTER 10

Life gradually got back to normal for Erica. When she was fully recovered from the ordeal she was put back to work, serving in the restaurant, required at all times to be naked save for her high heels and hold-up stockings so that the guests could see and examine her fading welts and perhaps so that fellow slaves could appreciate the folly of disobedience.

Occasionally someone would want to examine her in closer detail. One woman in particular was fascinated by the way Erica's skin was marked where the whip had struck hardest, stopping her in the passageway outside the restaurant and spending several minutes running her fingers over the ridges. After a few minutes the swing doors opened and they were joined by a distinguished grey-haired man, who Erica recognised as a television news broadcaster.

'I wondered where you'd got to,' he said to the woman. 'What are you up to?'

'Look, Ray, come and look at this,' the red-haired woman replied enthusiastically. Even though it was early she was dressed in a deep-blue satin evening dress, cut low enough to reveal a deep cleavage and slit up the line of one leg to the top of her thigh, showing just a glimpse of the dark band of her stocking top when she moved. The man studied Erica's back. 'Can I have her, please?' the woman implored.

Erica had a sudden sinking feeling in the pit of her stomach, thinking of how 21 had been taken away, almost certainly bought by some unknown person. Could this woman mean that? But then if so, would it be so bad? Perhaps if she was bought and taken away from *The Complex* she would stand a better chance of escape. At least the couple were English so it was unlikely she would be taken overseas.

The man looked her up and down. 'We're new here,' he said, 'our first time. Are you available?'

'Yes, Master, whatever you instruct,' Erica said, hating herself for her subservience.

'Anything?'

'Yes, Master.'

'You don't object if my lady friend wants you?'

'I am not permitted choices, Master.'

'And we can have you now, here, or we can buy you permanently, am I correct?'

Erica could feel her blood run cold. 'Yes, Master.'

'You want me to buy her for you, my pet?' the man asked. 'Or do you just want to have her for now?'

'Just for now,' the redhead cooed, slipping two fingers between Erica's legs and sliding them inside her. 'But if she's as good as she looks and feels I might want her permanently. She's very wet, Ray. I think she wants me too. Don't you want to watch me have her?'

'Where's your room, slave?' Ray asked Erica.

'Her name is 51,' the woman said, moving her free hand over the numbers adorning Erica's buttock.

Despite herself Erica said under her breath, 'My name is Erica.'

Ray sniggered. 'Oh, this is the one. I've heard of you.'

'What?' the woman demanded.

'Apparently she can be a bit of a rebel, this one,' he said. 'You know Laurence Pettinger, the MP?'

The redhead nodded. 'The one who was in all the news when his daughter disappeared? You mean this... this is her?'

'The very same,' Ray replied.

'But the newspapers said she was dead,' the woman purred, seemingly finding Erica even more interesting with this revelation. 'They even had a funeral for her.'

Erica's heart sank further. She had always clung on to the faint hope that someone, somewhere, was still looking for her. Now all hope was gone. The world no longer knew she existed.

'Well, slave, where's your room?' Ray asked again.

'This way, Master,' she said quietly, indicating the passage to their right.

'Well then, lead on,' he instructed, and Erica walked ahead, aware that the couple's eyes were watching her nakedness, but too weary with it all to protest. She had deserted her duties in the restaurant, but that was not her problem. The girls were not allowed choices like that. It was their prime directive, as the recently installed new Director had put it, to obey any of the guests regardless of what else they were doing at the time. So someone else would have to worry if they were shorthanded in the restaurant. With over seventy girls now in *The Complex* a replacement would soon be found.

As they approached her door she heard the familiar click as it unlocked and slid open. Her bed, as always, had been made by some unknown person. Erica entered and stood facing the foot of it, aware of the couple behind her.

'Can I do whatever I want with her?' the woman asked breathlessly.

'Apparently you can, yes,' the man replied. 'You heard what they said at the introduction gathering. We can do what we want, when we want. The slaves are, as they say, expendable. So what do you want to do with her?'

Without answering the woman walked over to where Erica stood, then slowly around her, looking her up and down. 'Kneel,' she instructed.

There was something in her tone that Erica did not like, and was even slightly afraid of. It was soft, almost casual, yet held an unmistakable menace. Erica immediately sank to her knees.

'She's obedient now, it seems,' the woman said, looking back at her partner. 'Want to watch me fuck her?'

'Sure I do,' he replied, moving over to the chair to the right of the bed. 'And you'll bring me off in her mouth after you have.'

The woman stared daggers at him. 'I'm not your slave!' she snapped vehemently, and at least Erica had stopped being the focus of attention for a moment as the man stood again, moving quickly across to the woman and twisting his hand into her hair, pulling sideways and down, making her gasp and snatch at his hand to stop the sudden pain. Erica kept looking at the floor, watching developments from the corner of her eye.

'Fuck you!' the woman cried. 'Get off!'

The man twisted his hand tighter in her hair and pulled her face to his. 'Let's not forget who's the boss here, slut!' he spat. 'You were in the gutter when I found you and I can put you right back there without a second thought.'

'All right, all right, I'm sorry,' she wailed, trying to stop his hand pulling her hair. Her previous elegance had gone, the slit in her skirt wide now, showing her black suspenders and the 'V' of her knickers as she struggled. To add to her humiliation the man reached up with his free hand to yank her neckline down, snapping the thin straps of her dress and exposing her ample breasts.

'You, 51,' he said suddenly, 'find some rope. You can help me teach this spoilt little bitch a lesson.'

'Yes, Master,' Erica said, standing and moving to the drawer unit beside the door, where all the paraphernalia of bondage and restraint were kept. She pulled out four of the neatly coiled white ropes and moved back to the feuding couple.

'Tie her hands behind her back,' he ordered. 'Make it good or you'll be sorry too.'

Erica dropped three of the ropes onto the bed before she uncoiled the fourth. The woman was still trying to tug the man's grip from her hair, but he was far too strong for her.

'Put your hands behind your back,' he told her.

'No!' she wailed.

His free hand flew to her chin and clamped her jaw roughly. His voice was calm, yet with unmistakable menace. 'Look, you're just as expendable as any of the slaves here. Now put your hands behind your back or I may decide to enrol you as an inmate.'

Her eyes stared venomously back at him, but slowly she realised he was serious and dropped her hands, moving them behind her so Erica could tie them. She knew well enough how to do it, since not many days went by when she wasn't bound in some way, and frequently she was required to assist in the subjugation of one of the other girls. Five times around the woman's wrists, crossover, pass the cinch loop through and back again, then securely knot the ends.

The man was looking around the room, spotting the winch hook in the ceiling above them. 'How do we get that down?' he asked, then there was a click and a mechanical whir as the hook started to lower. 'How...?'

Erica's eyes darted to the ever-watchful video camera.

'Ah, thank you,' the man called, amused.

'You're welcome,' came an equally amused male voice from the speaker.

'Do I get privacy if I want it, or do you watch everything?' the man asked.

'You can have privacy if you want it,' the voice told him. 'Just ask.'

Another click signalled the stopping of the hook. 'Attach the rope to it,' he told Erica, and when she had done so he asked for the winch to be raised, dragging the woman's arms up behind her and bending her forward as it did so. He released her hair and waited until she was gasping with the discomfort of the position, then called for a stop and some privacy.

'Ring the bell by the door if you want anything,' the voice informed him before silence fell.

The man moved behind the trussed woman, amused by her futile struggles.

'Are you going to apologise now?' he asked.

'What for?' she defiantly spat back.

He turned slowly to Erica. 'Do you have a cane?' he asked.

Erica moved once again to the drawer unit, returning moments later with a swishy school cane, which she handed to him. 'Pull up her dress,' he ordered, and Erica was beginning to enjoy herself; the woman had treated her like an object and now she was being humiliated in return. She bent to grasp the hem of the dress, lifting it up the woman's shapely legs to her waist, following the man's instructions to tuck the hem into the low back, leaving the woman's rear totally exposed.

'Pull her knickers down,' he continued, clearly wanting her humiliation to be complete, so Erica put her thumbs in the sides of the tiny black panties and lowered them to the woman's feet.

'I'll give you a choice, Beth,' the man then proceeded. 'Do you want 51 to cane you, or me?'

'What?' came the incredulous reply. 'Ray, please, we don't have to do this. Please, I'll do anything.'

'You should have thought of that before,' he countered. 'Now choose. Her, or me?'

The reply was quick. 'Her, not you.'

Maybe she had seen him use a cane before, and the idea that he could be brutal with it made Erica shudder. She hated the cane most of all. The man held it out to her.

'Make it hard,' he instructed her. 'If I don't think you're doing it conscientiously enough I'll do it to you instead. Understand?'

'Yes, Master,' Erica whispered anxiously, then moved behind the woman, the cane ready to strike the taut flesh of her bottom. She waited for the signal to begin.

'Unless, Beth...' he teased, 'how about you suck me off instead?'

'Yes, anything,' she gasped.

'No biting?'

'No, no, I promise.'

The man was already undressing. He glanced at Erica's face, taking in her expression before she averted her gaze. 'The slave looks disappointed, Beth,' he told the woman. 'I think she wanted to cane you.'

When he was naked and erect he presented his pulsing cock to the woman's mouth. She hesitated before sliding her rouged lips over him and sucking deep. The man gazed down at her face as he fucked it, pulling her hair to one side so as not to obscure his view. Erica watched the way her mouth struggled to contain his thrusts, and too late she realised he was now looking at her.

'You think you could do better, slave?' he asked. 'Answer me!' he snapped impatiently when she failed to reply.

'Y-yes, Master,' she blurted without thinking.

'Then come here and kneel,' he ordered smugly.

Erica placed the cane on the bed and knelt beside the woman, their faces mere inches apart. The man pulled out of the redhead's mouth and presented his glistening cock for her to suck. She obediently licked around the helmet, twisting her practised movements this way and that to give him pleasure. She had learned well during her time at *The Complex*. Slowly she drew him in, opening her mouth wide and making sure her teeth did not nip him. Lifting her head slightly she pushed forward until he could feel the head of his cock at the back of her throat. Then she opened her eyes wide and looked directly up into his as she swallowed it even deeper into her throat.

The man let out a strangled gasp. 'Oh, yessss... that's very good...' He inhaled deeply to calm his heightening excitement. 'Are you watching this, Beth? You see now how to suck a man's cock?'

'Bitch!' the redhead spat at Erica, and if Erica could have smiled she would have. She was actually going to enjoy caning the spoilt woman.

'Want to try again?' the man asked her, reluctantly pulling out of Erica's mouth. He did not wait for a reply, he just moved to Beth and fed his cock between her lips, shunting his hips as she valiantly tried to swallow him. Her eyes widened as he reached the back of her mouth and she fought the natural reaction to gag, and finally she could take no more, pulling her head back and spluttering as she half choked.

'Oh dear,' the man mocked, pulling away from her and sinking back into Erica's waiting mouth. 'Now make me come, slave,' he told her.

Erica was emotionless about it. She had no choices. If she had she would not obey. She did not enjoy it, she endured it. It was less unpleasant than a refusal would be, and a refusal would result in some kind of reprisal until she obeyed anyway. They knew she would break eventually and so did she, so it was simpler to just get on with it. And she had become a good actress; she could make each male believe theirs was the biggest and finest cock in *The Complex*.

She could not say she had no interest in the act at all, but it was usually an interest in avoiding pain and humiliation. And this time she had an extra motivation; she wanted to see Beth punished instead of her. So she sucked and licked and moaned and pumped her fingers up and down his shaft, and when he gurgled in the back of his throat before ejaculating deep into her mouth she made all the appropriately appreciative noises.

'Very good, 51,' he panted, when he had recovered somewhat. 'Very good indeed. I'll have you do that again sometime.'

'Thank you, Master,' she whispered meekly; well, it never did any harm to appear grateful.

'What did you think of that, Beth?' the man asked the sulking redhead.

'I think she's a bitch and when I get free I'm going to kill her,' she sneered.

Ray laughed. 'No, my vicious little pet, you'll do no such thing. One, you haven't the guts and two, I forbid it.' He helped Erica to her feet. 'Now, slave,' he said, 'have you any objection to caning Beth?'

'No, Master.'

Beth started to plead again. 'Why's that, 51?' the man asked, talking over her protests.

'Because I do as I'm told, Master,' Erica said.

'So if I tell you to cane her harder, you'll cane her harder?'

'Yes, Master.'

'Good. Pick up the cane, 51.'

Erica retrieved the implement from the bed and took her position behind Beth, slightly to her left. Ray sat in the chair, watching.

'Start now, 51,' he ordered. 'And keep going until I tell you to stop.'

'Ray, please...' the redhead started, but Erica's cutting stroke across her waiting cheeks stopped the words dead.

Erica kept going with regular strokes, varying the position slightly with each so as to make the woman's bottom red all over. Meanwhile Beth screamed and cried, so much so that Ray picked up her discarded knickers and stuffed them in her mouth. Erica noticed the look of hatred on Beth's face when she caught her eye. He did not miss it either.

'Stop,' he said suddenly, and the woman visibly relaxed. Ray moved to her face and twisted it up to his gaze, pulling the knickers from her mouth.

'Are you angry with me, Beth?' he asked.

'Yes,' she spat, before reconsidering. 'No, I...'

'You wanted this slave before. You still want her?'

'Untie me and I'll show you what I want to do to her.' The woman's voice was strained and tense because of the extreme position he had her in.

'Later, maybe. But you can't blame her; she's only doing as I tell her.' He turned to Erica. 'Hit her again, harder.'

Erica struck once, making the woman tense again and scream out loud.

'Bastard!' she growled through gritted teeth.

'Good, Beth. Direct your frustration at me, not 51. Who knows, you could be joining her in here soon.'

'You wouldn't.'

'You don't think?' He smiled. 'Don't test me, Beth.'

He let go of her chin and let her head fall back. 'Now,' he continued as he walked back to the chair by the bed. 'Be nice to her. You said you'd fuck her. I prefer to watch you suck her. 51, push the button.'

Erica moved to the door to press the button that would reconnect them to the control room.

'Yes?' the same disembodied voice asked.

'Lower the winch,' Ray told him, and immediately the motor whirred into action, lowering Beth's hands until she could stand straight again. As she did her dress slid back down her thighs, catching for a moment on the tops of her stockings before continuing its noiseless descent to her ankles.

Ray told Erica to unhook the winch and asked the man to raise it again, and when the whirring motor stopped he once again asked for privacy.

'Kiss each other,' he told the two females. Beth shot him an indignant glance again, and then lowered her gaze as he continued. 'Or I'll use the cane.'

Erica was unmoved. She kissed Beth on the lips, meeting a hard, tense, reluctant response.

'Do it, Beth,' he warned. 'I can assure you I cane far harder than this slave. You said you wanted her, so do it.' To emphasise his threat he moved to pick up the pliable implement.

'All right,' she said quickly. 'All right.'

So the two women kissed, both putting on their act to amuse and placate Ray, because both knew they had no other choice. Erica was surprised to find Beth quickly responsive, opening her mouth and pressing her tongue forward to engage her own, and then she chose her moment to viciously bite Erica's lower lip.

'Bitch!' she spat as Erica yelped and pulled away, raising her hand to her mouth and finding blood there.

Ray moved fast. 'I told you,' he said, bringing the cane down with force across Beth's back, making her legs buckle as she screamed out and sank to her knees.

'No, please!' she pleaded, and he calmed quickly.

'Beth,' he told her, his voice almost soothing. 'You still have choices and I suggest you use them wisely while you do. You can do as I say and later today we can go back to London, or you can continue to rebel, in which case I'll have no qualms at all about leaving you here to become one of the slaves. I could even suggest you share a room with your new friend, 51.' He thought for a moment before turning to Erica. 'How many slaves are there here now?'

'About 42 at the moment, Master, I think,' she replied uncertainly.

'And what's the name of the most recent?'

'I think it's 81, Master,' she answered, remembering the induction of a Japanese girl fairly recently.

'Well, Beth,' he resumed. 'You would become number 82.'

'No!' she quavered.

'And you could have the numbers tattooed into your skin like 51 has. Did it hurt?'

'Yes, Master,' Erica told him truthfully.

'Worse than any beating?'

'Perhaps, Master.'

'Did you pass out?'

Erica nodded, remembering the blackness that had descended on her moments after her own parents had pressed the wicked needles into her flesh.

'Now, what do you think?' he continued. 'Do you want to remain Beth, and retain all your freedoms, or do you want to become 82 and stay locked up here as a slave?'

'No, I'll do anything,' she sobbed, crying openly. 'Anything.'

'Good. Now, you're going to thank 51 for caning you by sucking her. Do you understand?'

She nodded meekly.

'And if you bite or do anything spiteful you become number 82. Now, have you got that?'

'Yes... I've got that.' She knew she was beaten.

Ray told Erica to get on the bed and spread her legs, and then instructed Beth to climb between them and do as she was told. Without her hands to support her, Beth's face pressed hard into Erica's crotch, but despite herself Erica responded to the woman's tongue as it separated her pussy lips and sought out her clitoris. Either Beth had done this before or she was a natural, and Erica settled back to get whatever enjoyment she could from the act. That's how she had become; resigned to the beatings and humiliation, taking what pleasure she could from life and waiting, waiting for the day she would get free.

Beth never did become 82. But she did become 83.

The number 82 was reserved for a tall, willowy blonde who, they were told at her induction, was consigned to *The Complex* on her eighteenth birthday by her stepfather, who was introduced to the diners. The man stood and waved a hand in acknowledgement. They were not often told of a slave's background, but for some reason the Director went to some lengths to explain this girl's past.

In the same way Erica had been when she had first arrived here, the blonde girl had her arms and legs strapped to the two vertical posts on the turntable in the centre of the stage. Unusually, she wore a T-shirt and jeans. She looked rebellious; staring back at the crowd with a fire that Erica knew only too well would soon be doused. The more defiant the slave was, the more sadistic pleasure they would take in her absolute subjugation.

They had all been called, as usual, to the packed restaurant and made to kneel in a row facing the stage during the induction ceremony. This was not the labelling ceremony; that would come later. This was an opportunity for the guests and the other slaves to meet the new inmate. For certain she would be humiliated and whipped, that happened every time. At some point in the ceremony all the slaves would be required to walk onto the stage and whip her too. It had happened at Erica's initiation and all the ones she had attended since. She had done it without malice or emotion. Better someone else than her. Noble gestures just brought more pain.

Erica, as with several of the other girls present, was shackled with loose chains attached to locked leather cuffs at her ankles, wrists and neck. It gave them sufficient freedom of movement to serve at the tables, yet not enough to protect themselves should one of the guests decide to use a whip or a cane on them.

The general murmur of conversation and the clattering of cutlery were constantly underlined by the jangling of chains as the slaves moved among the tables. Apart from the chains she was dressed, as instructed, in black underwear comprising a tiny see-through thong, wispy suspender belt and uplift bra. Black seamed nylons and high stilettos completed the outfit.

They were told the girl's father had left her and her mother when she was a baby, and that her mother had remarried soon after. Two years ago her mother died and she lived with her stepfather. Erica could imagine what that entailed. The stepfather had the sort of manner that made her think the new girl had probably been the target of his sexual attentions for some years.

Apparently for the last year the girl had become unruly and delinquent. She had run away a few times but he always found her. And then finally he snapped and decided to put an end to her rebellious behaviour. Her stepfather, they were told, was a judge. He knew people. As far as the world at large was concerned the girl had run away and he could not look for her any more. She would become another statistic. *The Complex* was full of such statistics.

From the corner of her eye Erica noticed the stepfather was accompanied by a female who did not look much over eighteen herself. No doubt the man had a new interest in his life and wanted his inconvenient stepdaughter out of the way. For good.

The man she only knew as the Director continued to speak, telling the girl the familiar facts that she was here for as long as they wanted her, that she was expendable, that she was required to obey any instructions from the guests without question, that she was not allowed to talk unless given permission and that if she needed to talk she must kneel and await permission.

Erica held her breath, as always willing the new girl to just agree, to avoid the inevitable punishments that would come from defiance. But it rarely happened.

'Fuck you!' the girl snarled, then louder, to the room, 'Fuck you all!' She focussed on her stepfather and his new girl. 'And most of all, *fuck you*...!' Her last two words were uttered with intense venom, so everyone knew he never had been a real father to her.

The reaction was obviously planned. A man and a woman stepped forward from the back of the stage. He held her face and pressed his finger and thumb into her cheeks, forcing her mouth open. She tugged uselessly at her bonds. The woman pressed a rubber ball-gag between her teeth and moved round to fasten the strap tightly behind her neck. When it was complete, both resumed their positions at the rear of the stage. Still the girl mumbled obscenities at the room, her eyes glowing with defiance.

'These are her favourite clothes, apparently,' the Director said into his microphone. 'Not very elegant, are they?' A few amused murmurs arose from the room. 'Scissors, please,' the man called, and the woman brought a pair forward for him, relieving him of his microphone.

He started at the bound and gagged girl's waist, cutting upwards from the hem, between her breasts to her throat, so that the fabric fell apart to reveal a white bra and tanned flesh. He continued to cut, to her left shoulder, down the arm, then again on the right, so that the shirt fell in tatters to the stage. She watched, mumbling curses at him, but taking care lest the sharp scissors should cut her.

When the shirt was a ruined rag around her feet, two quick snips severed her bra straps. He reached up with his left hand to pull the delicate cups away from her breasts before sliding the scissors between them to cut there too, and it quickly joined the ruined shirt on the floor.

The girl's breasts were as tanned as the rest of her, causing the man to comment. 'I'm assured the tan is genuine,' he smiled. '81 does like to be topless when she's abroad. And I suspect it's an all over tan.'

The comment produced some murmurs of approval from the onlookers. The girl shook her head as he reached for the waistband of her jeans to pull it away from her trim stomach.

'Hmmm,' the Director continued, as if they were in some macabre pantomime. 'I can't quite see. What shall I do?'

He crouched down and started to cut upwards from her left ankle, working up the front of the jeans until he reached the waistband, where he stopped, moving to repeat the exercise on the right leg. When he finished her tanned legs were visible through the ragged slits. The room hushed, waiting for the girl's body to be fully exposed. The man held the waistband of her jeans as he completed the cuts on both sides, finally letting it fall.

The girl looked good in her white panties, athletic and slim as she was.

'We still can't see, can we?' the man mocked, before gripping her dainty white underwear and tugging viciously, ripping them off completely and making her squeal into the rubber gag.

Her tan was not an all over one, the little white area of flesh now exposed indicating that her bikini was even more brief than her underwear.

He passed the scissors back to the waiting woman and took the microphone again. 'Ladies and gentlemen,' he announced. 'This is 82. She'll be whipped later, but in the meantime please enjoy her discomfort and your meals.'

Erica tried again to make visual contact with the girl, whose hate-filled eyes glared back at the room, her chest rising and falling as her anger made her breath struggle against the constriction of the gag. The girl's eyes moved along the line of kneeling slaves at the front of the stage, catching Erica's as she passed.

'Just do as they say,' Erica tried to silently mouth to her, but the girl's eyes moved on, then quickly glanced back, narrowing slightly as she tried to pick up the message. For a moment Erica thought she had got through, but as she watched the fire returned and the glance was lost. The girl did not look her way again, and the appearance of one of the male guests on the stage made Erica lower her face and stare at the floor once again. She hated herself for her lack of defiance. But it was useless. Defiance meant pain. There was nothing to gain from it, nothing at all. There was no law, no fairness, no reason. Only obedience and submission. Fighting meant losing, and losing meant punishment.

Nothing changed for perhaps half an hour. The girl stared with venom back at the room as the diners continued with their meals and their wine. A quartet played from the left of the stage, but were generally ignored as people chatted and laughed as if in any normal restaurant - except this one did not have waitresses, it had slaves.

'51!'

Erica's heart jumped as she heard her number called. The voice was female; she recognised it as Grace, one of the house Mistresses. She stood immediately and turned in the direction of it. The woman, in her mid-thirties, her dark-brown hair pulled back into a severe ponytail, held a silver tray with a bottle of port on it.

'Take this to table twenty-seven,' Grace told her. 'Remain there until dismissed, and then return to your position.'

Erica did not reply; she had not been told to. She simply took the tray and did as instructed, and it was only when she drew close that she saw who sat at table twenty-seven, and why she had been chosen to serve them. Watching her approach with obvious sadistic relish on his face, sat her stepfather, Laurence Pettinger MP. Erica felt the anger rising inside her again, fuelling her with enough energy and hatred to take the bottle and smash it over his loathsome head. But she knew that was exactly the kind of futile reaction he wanted and what the consequences would be, so she would not fall for such provocation. She was aware of her mother to his left, but the other couple present she had never seen before.

The man looked distinguished and gentle, but she would not let that fool her. This was no place for gentle men or gentlemen. His companion looked out of place, fairly heavy-set with short bobbed hair and a tawdry flower-print dress.

Erica put the tray on the table and stood back, trying hard to contain her rage.

'What do you think of her?' Laurence Pettinger was asking the other man.

'Very attractive,' the man said as he looked her up and down.

'Do you want her?' her stepfather asked.

Erica steeled herself.

'What, now?' the incredulous man retorted.

'If you want to. I told you, the slaves in this place are permanently available. You just tell them what to do and they do what you tell them.' He looked up into Erica's fiery eyes. 'It's my friend's first time here, slave,' he told her. 'So I want you to unzip his trousers and fellate him.'

Erica paused but a moment, ready to react mutinously, but she was not going to be beaten that easily; she knew what her stepfather was trying to do. So she sank to her knees beside the man, waiting while he turned towards her. She noticed his anxious glance at the woman, but it did not stop him facing her and it did not make him stop Erica as she leaned forward a little to slide down his zip. He was only half erect when she reached inside his trousers to fumble his cock into the open.

Her chains chinked quietly as she leaned further forward to take him into her mouth. She knew her mother and stepfather were watching and she closed her eyes to shut out what was happening, but a sudden swat across her bottom made her jerk and open them again.

'Keep your eyes open, slave,' her stepfather ordered. From somewhere he had produced a short riding crop, which he lashed across her bottom a second time to make his point. The man was fully erect now, staring down aghast to where over half his cock disappeared inside her lovely mouth.

'Is she good?' Laurence Pettinger asked his guest.

'Um, oh yes, amazing,' the man breathed.

'Do you know who she is?' her stepfather continued.

'Um, no, how could I?' he gasped.

'Remember all that media fuss some time ago when my *daughter* disappeared?'

'Yes,' the man said matter-of-factly. Then it sank in. 'You mean...? She's...?'

Laurence Pettinger chuckled. 'Oh yes. Now is that kinky or what?'

'So all the rumours about you are right, Pettinger,' the man said. 'You are a contemptible bastard.' But there was no disdain or disgust in the words or the tone. In fact the man was chuckling along with his lecherous host as his erection grew further in Erica's throat, and he moved his hand to the back of her head to press her down further onto him until he was penetrating her deeply.

'Is she performing diligently enough for you?' her stepfather asked.

'Yes indeed,' the man said, his voice growing huskier.

'And how's this feel?' Pettinger asked, emphasising the question with another swat of the crop across her vulnerable bottom.

'Very good,' the man enthused. 'Very different.'

Erica was vaguely aware that the noise around them had diminished as the nearby diners turned to watch her performance. Her stepfather continued to beat her poor buttocks as she sucked and the man kept his firm downward pressure on her head, occasionally allowing her to lift up only a few inches before he pushed her back down, her flushed face rubbing against the material of his trousers. Then an especially hard swat made her squeal around the cock plugging her mouth, extracting a deep hiss of breath from him too.

'Again, do that again,' he moaned. 'And you,' he cruelly twisted his fist in Erica's hair to stress his demand, 'don't you dare swallow until I say you can.'

Laurence Pettinger was more than happy to oblige, repeatedly striking hard so that Erica's muted squeals vibrated through the throbbing cock filling her mouth, and after a dozen or so stinging strokes the shuddering man clamped her head between his hands as he pumped his seed deep into her throat.

After a few moments he pulled her head up, twisting his wrist until she had to look into his face. 'Let me see,' he ordered. 'Open your mouth.' She meekly obeyed, exhausted by the ordeal, and he saw that his sperm still coated her tongue and teeth. 'Now swallow,' he said, smiling smugly at Laurence Pettinger, then back down at her lovely flushed face as her eyes closed and her throat convulsed.

'Let it trickle out now,' he told her.

Any contempt she held for him was completely overshadowed by the presence of her stepfather and her determination that some day she would wreak her revenge. She tilted her head forward until she felt the salty excess fluid escape her mouth and run down her chin, slowing for a moment before finding a path down her throat, cooling as it coated the upper slopes of her breasts.

'Now, get back to whatever it is you have to do,' the man ordered dismissively. 'But no wiping it off. Understood? You're a worthless whore and I want everyone to see my mark on you. Understand?'

'Yes, Master,' she managed to say.

She rose, turning to go, but had not moved a pace before she heard her stepfather's voice again.

'Erica,' he said calmly.

Now her hatred was complete. He had condemned her to this place to be completely depersonalised, to be a number not a name, a thing not a person, and now he chose to remind her of her given name. She stopped, still facing away from him.

'Erica,' he repeated. 'Turn around. Look at me.'

She turned slowly, her eyes not daring to meet his in case he saw the venom they contained.

'You still remember your name, then? Speak.'

'I am 51, Master,' she told him, determined he would never win. '51.'

'Call me that again,' he said.

'Master,' she repeated.

He was unzipping his trousers. Erica tensed. Surely he wouldn't! Not that. She could not do it, she just could not. But, as usual, he was just torturing her.

'Go and find me a slave,' he said. 'A particularly good one. Choose badly and I will have you flogged.'

'Yes, Master.'

Erica's choice probably did not matter. If her stepfather, or any of the other guests for that matter, wanted her flogged, then she would be flogged, but she decided to do her best to appease him. She moved to the front of the stage again, walking to 43, a tall Jamaican girl whose skin contrasted so beautifully with her own, a fact often taken advantage of by guests who wanted to watch the pair perform lesbian sex for their amusement.

Since speech was not allowed she tapped the girl on the shoulder and signalled to her to rise. 43 formed a perfect contrast, dressed in the exact complement of Erica's clothes, with white underwear, stockings and shoes against Erica's black. She took the girl's hand and wove her way back through the tables to her stepfather. He looked 43 up and down as they approached, apparently pleased with her choice.

What followed was an almost exact repeat of her own recent experience with her stepfather's friend, and soon his sperm was running down 43's exposed breasts just like the other man's had on hers.

'Stand,' her stepfather told the coloured girl. 'Now kiss my daughter.'

The girl did not pause or falter and Erica found herself kissing another female, her own stepfather's semen still all too evident on the other's face, lips and tongue. She knew even that was meant to humiliate her and she again wondered what she had ever done to make her parents hate her so much.

'You can return now, we have no more use for either of you. Go!' her stepfather told them as a final dismissal.

They walked back through the tables, side by side, and 43 managed to whisper, 'I'd kill him.'

'I intend to,' Erica whispered back.

When they arrived back at the stage, two men were walking round the new girl, touching her where they wanted, inciting her to further anger. Erica did not even try to make contact any more; the girl was lost to her own fate. The question was not whether she would break, but simply how long she would last before she did. Erica watched as a bead of sweat ran down her face and dripped to her breast. Eventually the Director returned to the stage and called for silence. He unfastened the ball-gag and tossed it aside before smiling at the new girl.

'Still feeling defiant?' he asked her.

'Fuck you,' came her answer.

'Very well, let nobody say you didn't have a chance. Grace, a crop I think.'

The housemistress mounted the stage and walked to the cupboard all the slaves knew only too well. It contained dozens of implements whose sole purpose was to cause pain or humiliation... or both. 82 could not yet see what was intended for her. Until the Director flicked a button on the remote control so that the platform on which she stood started to rotate slowly, turning her to face the rear of the stage and exposing her bare back and bottom cheeks to the hushed diners. As she turned she noticed the crop in Grace's hands.

'W-what are you going to do?' she stammered.

'I already told you,' the Director said. 'You're going to be whipped. These slaves kneeling by the stage will be the first. They've been through it too, every one of them. But do not imagine that will make them more merciful; they all know better than that. Don't take it to heart either; just because they hurt you doesn't mean they have anything against you. In time, you'll understand.'

He nodded to Grace, who walked to the left end of the row of kneeling girls and beckoned them all to rise. She handed the crop to the first girl and stood aside for her to mount the stage. She was a striking Japanese girl called 28, and she walked to the new girl and waited for the signal to begin.

'Proceed,' the Director told her when the room was completely quiet.

She raised the crop and swiped it hard across 82's back. The swish was followed instantly by the crack as leather lashed flesh and immediately by the scream from 82. The Japanese girl walked back to her place and handed the crop to the next girl, ready for the whole sequence to be repeated. Eventually it was Erica's turn. 82 was already sobbing and pleading by that time, but Erica had to ignore it. She aimed for a part of her back that was not already marked by the crisscrossed red welts and struck hard. Any sign of leniency would be punished, something none of the girls wanted to risk.

Long before the last girl had her turn 82 had passed out. But that did not stop the ritual.

CHAPTER 11

Beth appeared at her own ritual some time later. Despite their previous conflict, Erica took no pleasure from her submission and the accompanying whipping.

Ray was there to witness it, and in fact insisted on giving the first cut of the crop, which he did with all the force he could muster, making even Erica wince. Beth cried throughout, begging to be set free, but she was wasting her breath appealing to anyone's better nature. The more desperate the girls got the more the sadistic guests and controllers enjoyed it. After the ritualised whipping from all the girls Beth was taken away to her room and Erica was appointed to visit her.

It was the first time she had ever been given that task, though she remembered well how it had happened to her. She was to educate Beth, or 83 as Erica would now have to call her, in the ways and the rules of *The Complex*. If Beth reacted badly or disobeyed she would be beaten, but Erica would be held to blame and would be beaten too. She had no doubt it was Ray who made the choice, since the two females already held a grudge between them.

Beth had been back in her room for ten minutes or so when Erica was taken there. The dislike showed as soon as she entered, but since Beth had been chained by her collar to the bed there was no way she could physically reach Erica, who waited out of reach, silent, since she had not been given permission to speak. Whoever was watching and listening in the control room waited too, perhaps amused by Beth's reaction to the presence of Erica in her room.

'This is all your fault!' she spat, tugging uselessly at the chain. 'Let me out of here, you bastards!' she shouted at the camera.

'83, sit on the bed, now!' came the controller's voice.

'Fuck you!' Beth called in response.

The voice was calm and slightly amused. 'We can wait longer than you, 83. Think about the beating you just received. Think how easily it can be repeated.'

Beth mellowed instantly. 'No, please, I...'

'51 is not your enemy. Nor is she your friend. She just *is*. Revenge will not be tolerated unless we allow it. You have to get used to your slavery, 83. All the slaves do as they're told. If I tell 51 to cane you, she'll cane you. If I tell her to kiss you, she'll kiss you. Isn't that right, 51? Speak.'

'Yes, Master.' Erica's ever-present yearning to rebel would stay under the surface for now.

'Which would you prefer, 83, a kiss or a caning?' Beth did not respond. 'Answer, 83, or we'll punish you anyway.'

'A kiss,' the woman said hastily.

'Louder.'

'A kiss!'

There was a pause, and Erica imagined they were discussing whether to allow it.

'51, kiss her,' the order finally came.

Erica advanced, aware of the other woman's seething anger, and as she got within reach Beth slapped her across the face. Erica reeled back, but was not about to be deterred. The punishment for disobeying was far worse than anything Beth could dish out. Her next approach was met with a similar assault, as was the third, the repeated slaps making her a little dizzy.

'Back off and wait, 51,' the controller finally intervened, and as Beth stood glowering at her, her breasts rising and falling as she fumed, Erica knew only too well what would happen next. She did not flinch when she heard the door click open behind her, but Beth did, suddenly looking fearful as two men entered. They moved quickly and efficiently, fitting metal cuffs to Beth's wrists before unfastening the collar and positioning her in the middle of the room. Then the winch lowered and one of the men raised her arms and hooked it to her cuffs.

'No, please,' Beth suddenly begged. 'You can't do this to me, please.'

But the men took no notice and the winch started again, rising back towards the ceiling as Beth pleaded to be released, soon finding herself stretched up on tiptoe, vulnerable and exposed. Though Erica disliked Beth she felt sorry for her, remembering the days when she had rebelled with such soul-destroying futility.

'Now, 83,' said the controlling voice, 'have you learned obedience yet?'

'Yes, yes I have,' she gabbled desperately.

'Do you still hold any grudges against 51?'

After a pause Beth managed a strained, 'No.'

'Good, we're glad to hear it. So now you may talk to each other, on any subject apart from personal details. We will be listening.'

The speaker clicked off. Neither of them said a word at first, before Erica tentatively broke the silence. 'I don't have anything against you, 83. I just do as I'm told and you have to do the same. They will always punish you if you don't. You can't win, so you just have to accept, obey, and do your best to keep your head down.'

'But how could Ray do this to me, put me in a place like this?' Beth sobbed.

'I don't know.' Erica suddenly felt sympathy for her, understanding exactly what betrayal felt like.

'But now I'd better tell you a few rules,' she went on, changing the subject, 'for your own good. You're not allowed to speak unless they permit it, and if you need to speak to a Master or Mistress you have to approach them, kneel on the floor with your head bowed and wait for him or her to give you permission. You have to do what they say when they say it, and believe me it's not worth resisting.'

'How many Masters and Mistresses are there?' Beth asked.

'I've no idea, but it's a lot. You may well recognise some of them from public life.'

'So what kind of things might I have to do... you know... *sexually?*' Beth asked timidly.

Erica shrugged. 'Anything they tell you.'

'Like what?' Beth needed to know. 'I'm not that experienced.'

'Straight, oral, anal, masturbation, objects... you name it. With men and with women, sometimes a few at a time.' Erica gave her a puzzled look. 'But I don't understand, 83; when you came in that first time you said you were going to fuck me. That doesn't sound like an inexperienced girl.'

'I... I was trying to impress Ray,' she admitted. 'I didn't want him to get bored with me.'

'Just how much sexual experience have you had?'

'Not much. The man's always done all the work. Before that session with you I'd only ever been with three men, and none of them were very spectacular, either.'

'Do you like giving oral sex?'

Beth screwed her face up. 'Not much,' she said. 'And I've always refused to swallow.'

'God, they'll love you,' Erica said hopelessly.

'What do you mean?'

'They'll make you do it and they'll come in your mouth too, or anywhere else they want, for that matter. So what about anal?'

Beth looked shocked and disgusted. 'I've never done that, and I don't intend to either!'

Suddenly the door clicked and opened on its motorised hinges. Two different men entered; Erica had seen both before. The winch clicked on and lowered Beth's feet to the floor and one released her wrists.

'So,' the taller one said menacingly, 'you've not had anal and no man's come in your mouth?'

'No,' Beth said naively, and Erica glared at her. 'No, Master.'

'Well all that's about to change,' he grinned.

'N-no, please,' Beth stuttered, already backing off, but there was nowhere to go. They grabbed an arm each and manhandled her to her hands and knees as she looked up at Erica, pleading for help Erica was unable to give.

When she was on all fours they let go, taking their time undressing, folding their clothes neatly, almost ceremonially, on the bed. Then they moved to her and sank to their knees. The shorter one gripped her hair and twisted, making Beth gasp, immediately using the opportunity to sink his cock into her mouth.

The other waited until his associate had set up a rhythm in and out of her mouth before pushing two fingers into her pussy and spreading the lubrication around the entrance to her rectum. When ready he shuffled forward to press his cock to her tiny puckered opening, then gripping her hips he tensed his buttocks and pushed steadily. Erica watched Beth's mouth snatch back from the erect cock to scream as the second pushed smoothly, completely, home.

The first man did not allow any respite for long, pulling her head back down and thrusting in deep. Beth was not allowed to utter any more protests, though Erica could see she wanted to. Each thrust from the man deep in her anus made her eyes widen and her face wince, tears meandering down her cheeks as she sobbed.

Erica could do nothing but wait and hope and be glad it was not her at the centre of the two men's drooling attention.

The taller man was holding Beth by her waist now as he thrust faster and faster into her, while the other held her head still as he too gathered speed between her stretched lips. The tall man came first, pushing deep and staying still as he emptied into her, then moments later the other man threw his head back and pumped his seed into her instinctively gulping throat.

'Swallow,' he told her. 'Swallow it or I'll spank you.'

Beth did as she was told, and satisfied they pushed her to the carpet, where she sobbed as she strove to come to terms with the treatment she had suffered. Barely noticed by her the men dressed again and left the tense atmosphere of the room.

'What's your name?' the voice wanted to know, then waited patiently.

Eventually Beth whimpered, '83...'

'Have you any other names?'

Beth wearily shook her head. 'No, none... Master.'

'51, help 83 to bed.' The voice seemed to mellow, just a little. 'And 51, you may sleep here tonight.'

CHAPTER 12

Beth soon learned not to hate the others. There was no point. Erica explained it all to her. But she still clung on to hope - hope that this was all some awful dream from which she would awake safe at home, or perhaps some cruel practical joke played on her by Ray and that he would appear at any moment, laughing, and take her away again.

But she never awoke from a dream, and Ray never came back for her. She saw him often, but he never spoke to her or showed her any tenderness. He would go out of his way to humiliate her at first, making her perform sexual acts with other men or women, always choosing her as his personal waitress while he fucked other slaves, making her watch in silence.

But after a while that stopped too. He did not even care about her enough to humiliate her any longer.

The friendship between Beth and Erica grew. They would even silently mouth each other's names when they were sure no video camera could see them, a shared secret that cemented the sisterhood. When required to have sex with each other they would get some pleasure from giving to each other, and even when they had to punish each other they resolved not to let it affect them.

It was always going to be noticed, of course. They knew it would be sooner or later. Maybe they were careless, or complacent, or maybe a video camera was hidden where they had not noticed, but their time had come. The controllers could not allow friendships between slaves.

Erica was locked in her room, recovering from a long session with a retired jockey who, dressed in his full riding gear, had her on her hands and knees while he sat astride her back and beat her bottom with a crop. He had not wanted anything else; no sex, nothing, just to have her be his mount while he flogged her, pulling on the bit between her teeth to steer which way she crawled.

He was only small but she was exhausted by the end of it. He even paid her a compliment of sorts, saying she had been the best horse he'd had and that he would ride her around the grounds very soon.

The clicking of the door awakened her, but she was too tired to move. She opened her eyes lazily as the two men approached the bed and fitted shackles to her wrists, pulling her to her feet as soon as they were locked.

One man fitted a leash to the ring in her collar as the other crouched to fasten the leg shackles to her ankles. The chain between them would allow her to walk with small, shuffling steps. He fitted another chain to join her wrists to her ankles, and then pushed a rubber ball-gag into her mouth. Erica adjusted her lips as best she could to accommodate it as he buckled the strap at the back of her head, and once completed they led her, naked, from the room.

Outside in the corridor stood two more men, one of them holding a leash attached to Beth's collar, who stood identically shackled and similarly naked.

Erica's leash was handed to the man who held Beth's, and he led them forward as the other three men walked off in the other direction. The chains jangled as the two females moved side by side, glancing at each other to see if they had any clues as to what was going on.

They stopped outside a room Erica had never been to before, the man knocking on the door and waiting until a small individual in a white coat answered it. He stood back, bowing his balding head slightly as he let them enter. The man holding the leashes jerked them forward, Beth staggering slightly as she lost her footing.

The whole atmosphere of the room made them feel uneasy. The three hospital beds arranged in a neat row along one wall each had a crisp white sheet covering most of the sterile black covers. Beside each stood an ordered table containing stainless steel dishes and surgical equipment in sealed plastic wrappers. A nurse in full uniform stood to their right.

Beth took one look and started to complain from behind the gag, vainly pulling away and trying to get to the door. The man holding the leashes separated them and pulled her forward. Erica knew the futility of trying to escape. She knew that whatever was about to happen was inevitable, so she stood still as the man dragged Beth back and forced her down onto the nearest of the beds and strapped her down.

When Beth was secure he turned to Erica and nodded his head towards the centre bed. Erica's chains chinked quietly as she walked the few paces forward and waited while he unfastened her shackles. She sat on the bed and settled back, watching as he strapped her arms and legs to the metal frame, finishing with a strap across her waist and another across her throat. Satisfied with his work, the man checked Beth's straps again and left the room.

Erica assumed the balding man was some kind of a doctor. He called the nurse to Beth first and she clicked forward on high heels - impractical for a nurse, but nothing here was ever normal or sensible - carrying a kidney-shaped dish of instruments. Erica twisted her head towards the struggling Beth to see what their fate would be.

The doctor did not hesitate, swabbing Beth's breasts and nipples with surgical spirit before taking a long needle from the tray to push through Beth's right nipple. Erica felt nauseous as Beth cried out helplessly. He left the needle in place while he quickly repeated the operation with the other breast, then took it in turns twisting both round and through before replacing each of them with a gold sleeper ring.

She watched as the nurse and doctor moved to her side, fighting back the nausea, ignoring Beth's sobbing to her right. She closed her eyes and waited for the pain. Why did it always have to be pain? She tensed as the coldness of the spirit swab was wiped across her skin, and then gritted her teeth to await the needles. To her surprise it was not all that painful.

The doctor worked with practiced efficiency, completing the job in a matter of seconds, then once done the pair left the room, closing the door behind them.

'May we talk, Master?' Erica called to the inevitable cameras.

'You may, 51. Usual rules.'

'Are you OK?' Erica whispered to Beth.

'Why are they so cruel to us?' Beth asked plaintively.

'That's what gets them off, I suppose,' she replied. 'You can't fight it, it just makes them worse.'

'W-what else are they going to do to me?' Beth was still shaking and sobbing.

'Anything they want. Just don't fight them; they get more pleasure if you do, and it only works out worse for you in the end.' Erica paused, wanting to get off the subject before the listeners decided to punish her for her views. Ironically she knew she was being more rebellious by not fighting them. They wanted the slaves to fight, wanted to break them again and again, and her resigned acceptance annoyed and frustrated them. 'That didn't hurt as much as I thought it would.'

'No, I suppose not,' Beth agreed weakly. 'But I feel so used. What happens now?'

'I've no idea,' Erica told her frankly. 'We wait, I suppose.'

'For how long?'

'Until they decide we stop waiting. Just don't fight them.'

'Will we ever get out of this place?' Beth's tone sounded desperate, broken.

'Don't even think about it. Don't dream, don't hope. Just do what they tell you. It's the only way to survive in here.'

'I'm not sure I want to survive if this is all I've got to look forward to.'

Erica's reply was stern. 'Don't talk like that. If they hear you they'll *really* make your life hell. Believe me, it can get much worse than this.'

Erica stopped talking as the door opened, and framed in the light from the corridor was a silhouette she recognised immediately - her stepfather, and right behind him stood Ray. Erica felt her fury mounting and fought to keep control. It was another of his sadistic games and it was one, for the moment, she could not win. Her stepfather walked to the side of her bed while Ray moved to the side of Beth's.

'Are you all right?' he had the nerve to ask.

Erica fought down her anger. 'As if you care.'

Laurence Pettinger smiled down at her. 'Still the rebellious little brat, aren't you?' he smirked.

'Go to hell!' Erica snarled back at him through gritted teeth.

'I can have you whipped for that.'

'I know,' she said flatly. 'You have many times already.' She refused to let him defeat her, no matter what the consequences, and he sensed her defiance.

'You can't win this, 51.' He had tried that one before, not even using her real name.

'Nor can you, Laurence Pettinger, MP,' she countered. 'What's the worst you can do to me? Kill me? I don't much care either way.'

She could see she was getting to him, his neck tensing as he fought to contain his anger. Then he seemed to come to a decision, reaching for his tie and slipping it off. Ray, meanwhile, had taken his place in an armchair, a thin smile on his face as he watched the proceedings unfolding. Pettinger did not stop until he was naked, and Erica felt the nausea rising again. Surely he wouldn't? Not her own stepfather. She trembled as he moved into the space between the beds.

'What about your friend here?' he goaded. 'Do you care about her particularly?'

'She's not my friend,' Erica said. 'She's just another slave, like me.' She knew this was dangerous ground. If her stepfather had been briefed by the control room he would know she was lying.

With cold, unflickering eyes on Erica, Pettinger deliberately cupped three fingers and pushed them roughly into Beth's pussy, making her gasp with the suddenness of it. His challenging stare never left his bound stepdaughter.

'Are you sure?' he growled. 'Perhaps if you stop lying to me I'll leave her alone. But then again, if you don't...'

As his voice tailed off he clenched his fingers, making Beth whimper and jerk on the bed. Erica dared not show any concern; it would just be worse for both of them.

'Do what you want to her,' she said as firmly as she could. 'At least it gives me some peace.'

'OK,' he sniggered, 'I will.'

Quickly he mounted the bed and fed his erection into Beth. Her body jerked as he rutted in and out and her breath came in gasping bursts as if being forced from her lungs.

Erica did not want to watch, but she could not tear her eyes away either. She thought he would surely come inside her friend, but with some apparent effort he stopped and rested.

'Ray, my dear fellow,' he said breathlessly, 'would you do me the honour of fucking my daughter?'

Erica had not really been aware of Ray undressing, yet when he appeared at her side he was as naked as her stepfather was. There was no foreplay, no consideration for her comfort, he just climbed between her legs and pushed his cock into her.

The two men watched each other as they picked up a similar rhythm. Erica felt cold and emotionless. She turned her head to look at Beth, noticing the tracks of glistening tears down her cheeks. Erica wished she could cry too, but she had forgotten how to.

As both men neared their climaxes Laurence Pettinger pulled out of Beth and stood between the beds, taking his erection, glistening from Beth's juices, in his left fist while he plucked a black rubber ring from one of the metal dishes. Then pumping his cock determinedly he forced the ring between Erica's lips, parting them wide, pushed his cock into the round opening and emptied his balls into her throat. And then as the loathing overtook her she was vaguely aware of Ray's grunts as he pumped his seed deep into her pussy, moments before she passed out.

For some time the same nurse attended Erica, bathing her nipples and twisting the sleepers to keep the piercings from healing. She never spoke to Erica at all, not a single word in the conversational sense. Erica was told to 'sit' or 'keep still', and that was it. She assumed the nurse was trained, yet how could she care for people and still witness the cruelty of *The Complex?*

Soon there was little discomfort and at least it meant the Masters and Mistresses left her breasts alone until they healed. Thankfully, for a while there were no sex and no punishments, though she worked long hours in the restaurant and serving drinks in the gardens.

Most of the time she had to wear the familiar shackles joining her ankles to her wrists, and her clothing varied between elegant evening dresses and flimsy underwear, from tiny thongs to panties with bras, suspenders, corsets, and slips. Each day she wore a special band around her upper left arm to inform the guests that she had been recently pierced, though whether that was to give them the opportunity to examine the sleepers or to warn them away from causing her damage, she never found out.

One day the nurse did not arrive at the expected time. Instead Grace, the housemistress, opened the door and walked into Erica's room.

'Stand, 51,' she said as the door slid silently shut behind her. 'Have you wondered why you had your nipples pierced? You may speak.'

'No, Mistress,' Erica said honestly. 'Just because someone decided it, I imagine.'

'Not quite,' the woman told her, craning her head forward slightly to look at the sleepers. 'There's another reason. But you're to have new rings fitted first.'

As always, right on cue, the door clicked open again and a man she had never seen before entered. He wore a white coat just as the doctor had, and Erica shrank back at the sight of him. He was small and timid, moving to the bedside table with shuffling feet and opening a case on its polished surface.

'Over here, on the bed,' he muttered, though Erica could not be sure whether he was giving her an order or telling Grace where she should go. She glanced at Grace.

'You heard him,' the woman said. 'On the bed. Sit.'

When seated, the man unfastened the sleeper in her left breast and took it out, placing it in his case. Erica had always been proud of her breasts, yet the little man did not seem at all moved by them, or even aware they were beautifully ripe breasts he was handling at all. He quickly removed the other sleeper and placed it with the first, before opening a small box to remove a pair of gold rings about an inch in diameter. He threaded them through her nipples in turn, pushing the joints together loosely. Once in place, he took from his bag a tiny butane torch and what looked like two grey flannels with a small slit in the centre of each. Erica gasped at the sight of the torch, wondering what torture this was.

'Heat-proof,' the nervous man explained, indicating the two squares of material. 'So you don't get burned.'

He pushed a cloth over each ring so it rested on her breast, and then screwed clamps in place on either side of the joins to shunt the heat away from her nipples. Lighting the blowtorch he adjusted the flame until it was a narrow blue spear, and then applied it quickly to the joint of the ring piercing her left nipple.

'Can you get me a wet cloth please, Grace?' he asked as he worked. 'Use cold water.'

Erica watched Grace go to the bathroom and return moments later with the wet flannel. He took it from her and moved the blowtorch away from the ring, pressing the cloth in place where he had worked. It hissed slightly as it cooled the hot metal, and water dripped onto her thighs.

A few moments later and he had repeated the exercise on the other ring. When it was cold too he removed the cloths and inspected his work.

'The only way they'll come off now is with a cutter,' he smiled at Grace.

Both females waited as he packed his case and left, and when the door was shut again Grace reached in her pocket for a gold chain with clip fasteners at each end and a ring in the centre. She clipped each of the fasteners to Erica's nipple rings and hooked her finger into the centre ring.

'Follow me,' she said, as if Erica had any choice, and moved her to stand beneath the ceiling winch, the chain of which started to lower immediately. Grace went to the drawer unit by the door to select a set of steel handcuffs. She efficiently snapped one on Erica's left wrist and moved behind her to snap the other to her right. Whatever was to happen, Erica's hands would play no further part.

'Your stepfather has ordered all this,' Grace said. 'He told us how you used to keep them up all night, wondering when, or even if, you were going to come home from yet another debauched night on the tiles.'

'They never waited up for me,' retorted Erica without thinking, only to be stopped short with a stinging slap across her face.

'Nobody gave you permission to speak, 51!'

Grace snapped the winch hook to the ring at the centre of Erica's breast chain, calling for it to be raised again, quickly stopping it when it was level with her breasts, so the chain hung loosely in front of her.

'You'll be fed later, 51,' Grace told her as she turned to leave. The door opened for Grace's exit and slid silently and solidly shut after she had gone. Erica did not understand at first. There was no discomfort, no pain, so what was her torture to be? Boredom?

After a short time standing there she was indeed bored, and Erica discovered what her torture was to be. Her feet ached from standing in one place for so long and her legs started to become restless. She moved around as much as she was able, but that was not much before the winch chain tightened and started to pull at her nipples.

That all meant she could not relax; she had to stand still and wait - but for how long? It also meant she was unable to sleep, and the realisation of that alarmed her. If she did she would fall and if she fell the rings would rip through her poor nipples. So she had to stay awake until they released her. So that was what Grace had meant - her stepfather was taking cruel revenge for the times she apparently kept him and her mother awake when she was enjoying yet another night out.

Some time later Beth arrived with her food and, watched by Grace, she stood and fed her friend with a spoon. Neither was permitted to talk. Once Erica had been fed she was left alone again, getting more and more tired. She closed her eyes a few times and saw herself as a child, running free through the meadows in Wales where she used to go to visit her grandmother.

Her imagination looked down at her feet, where her favourite white sandals skipped over the lush green grass, and she saw her lovely white dress with the bright red and yellow flowers decorating it. The sense of freedom was blissful, but all too short as sudden pain reminded her that she had started to droop.

Erica snapped her eyes open again, looking around the darkening room, the lights having been dimmed. From her first day at *The Complex* the light in the room had been kept constant, with one level when she was awake and a dim level when she was sleeping. The light and dark did not follow the patterns of day or night at first, because they wanted to destroy her sense of time. But this was different. The lights were being dimmed almost until she could not see the door. They wanted her to feel sleepy. They wanted to test her, to see what she could endure.

Then, unexpectedly, Grace's voice purred hypnotically from the speakers.

'You could try begging, 51. It might work.'

'Please let me go, I'll do anything,' Erica whispered, her mouth dry. She had little pride left, so she could beg. She *would* beg.

'That's no good, 51. We can make you do anything anyway. Try again.'

'Please, tell me what you want.'

She recognised the voice of her stepfather as he took over.

'Tell me you love me, Erica.'

That snapped her awake. He used her name. Was this to be an end to her ordeal, or even her time at *The Complex?* Was it possible he had punished her enough and was prepared to accept her again, to set her free?

'I... I love you,' her survival instincts forced her to say.

'What would you do to be set free, Erica?' he asked. 'Would you promise to behave yourself?'

'Yes, yes, anything.' Her pulse raced with the possibility that she could be on the verge of being freed.

'Would you promise never to tell anyone about this place?'

'Yes, I promise! Please take me away from here!' She was sobbing now with cautious euphoria.

'Prove it to me, Erica. Ask me to beat you now.'

'Please beat me, I want you to,' she pleaded. 'Now, please...'

His voice had become all there was in the world. If it meant freedom he could beat her. She knew she could take it.

'Very well,' he mused. 'Very well, I will.'

Erica stood upright, the tears streaming down her cheeks. She would take her beating. She wanted it. She needed it. All pride, all hatred, were gone. If he set her free he would become her hero. She would forgive all he'd had done to her. She would be his slave forever.

After a few minutes he strode through the opening door, a single-tailed whip in his right hand. 'You do want this, don't you?' he said.

'Yes, please... I need it,' she answered him, turning her back, presenting her flesh for his pleasure. Without hesitating he drew back and hit her hard, stinging her flank with the lash.

'Do you want more, Erica?' he asked.

'Yes, more, as much as you want,' she panted, so he struck her again and again.

'You're not crying, Erica.'

'I am,' she sobbed. 'Look.' She turned her face and showed him her tears.

'I want to hear you scream, Erica.'

She turned her back again and he resumed, swiping the whip down with such force it propelled her forward, forcing her to repeatedly shuffle back to stop the chains pulling her nipples with excessive pain.

Then suddenly the excruciating assault stopped, leaving her bathed in perspiration, her breasts rising and falling rapidly as she breathed deeply and absorbed the hurt.

'If I unchain you will you want more punishment?' he asked.

Erica nodded. 'Yes...' she whispered wearily.

Laurence Pettinger quickly unfastened the handcuffs and unclipped the chain from the winch. 'Bend over, Erica,' he growled, 'and present your bottom to me.'

Erica did as he ordered, gripping her ankles as she bent down to accept his gifts of pain. During the ongoing whipping she cried out, all attempts to keep it inside, to not be broken, gone. When the onslaught ceased for a moment she straightened up stiffly and turned to face him, begging him to whip her belly, thighs and breasts. When he stopped again, tired from his exertions, and sat in the chair to rest, she sank to her knees and dropped her head to his feet.

'Will you suck me willingly, Erica?' he asked, his voice a little strained.

She did not answer, for no answer was needed. She reached for the zip of his trousers and unfastened them, drawing him out and sinking her mouth over his throbbing erection. She closed her eyes and sucked the cock of her saviour. He was about to set her free, so at that moment she was willing to do anything to please him.

'And will you fuck me willingly?' he asked, after watching her working deliciously on his cock for some minutes.

Again she did not answer, but stood and straddled his thighs. As she lowered her pussy over his cock she felt she had forgiven him completely. The fact that he was the very reason she was here was suddenly unimportant, and all that was left was the fact he was going to take her away again. She kissed him deeply, using all her skills to give him a fuck to savour.

She rose and fell, she used her pelvic muscles to squeeze him, drawing him inexorably towards his climax, and when she felt him jerk and start to pump into her it triggered her orgasm too.

'Ohhhh,' she sighed blissfully, 'I love you.' Nothing mattered at that moment, not who he was nor who he had been. She sank over him, calm and peaceful for the first time in years, perspiration running between her breasts and coating her toned thighs with a healthy sheen. His hand stroked her hair as she rested.

'Let me up,' he said at last. She stood, and he did too, zipping himself up and dabbing sweat from his brow with a crisp white handkerchief.

'Come with me,' he told her as he moved towards the door. It opened and she followed as he started down the corridor. A group of men stood near the control room further along, with Grace to their left. Erica prayed she would never see any of them again. She wondered if her stepfather would give her something to wear for the journey home, but she did not care that much. If he wanted her naked she would be naked. She would walk all the way behind the car if he told her to.

Laurence Pettinger stopped in front of the group of controllers. 'Blindfold her, please,' he told Grace.

That made sense, Erica thought. They would not want her able to see her journey home. *Home*, the very word thrilled her. She stood still as Grace fitted the blindfold.

'Right,' her stepfather said when it was done, 'I have no more use for her. Do what you want. Sell her if you like. Goodbye, 51, we'll not meet again.'

Hands grasped her wrists as his words sank home.

'No!' she screamed, realisation plummeting in her stomach and making her feel horribly nauseous. 'No! You promised! I'll do anything for you, remember?'

Erica felt ropes being bound tightly around her wrists as she heard her stepfather's parting words.

'We have a new daughter now, 51.'

At that moment he lost her, forever.

CHAPTER 13

Erica was left on her bed, crying inconsolably. The blindfold soon slipped, leaving her to see the merciful darkness of her room. She lay on her side, arms bound tightly behind her back at the wrists and elbows, and legs bound together at the knees and ankles. She felt no discomfort and made no attempt to struggle. All the pain was inside. He had abandoned her again, but this time he had gone out of his way to give her some hope first. He deliberately set her up and she went along with it like a dumb fish caught on a line.

She did not care about the listening microphones or the watching cameras; they could give her no greater punishment than this. She spoke aloud, telling her room how sad she was, how she hated him, how she would be avenged.

The listeners let her ramble. Maybe, just maybe, they had some compassion for her. Or maybe they were enjoying her suffering. Erica did not care either way. Eventually she fell asleep.

She awoke slowly, her arms numb from the bonds. Someone was speaking to her, a gentle female voice, and a hand was stroking her hair. She opened her eyes to see Grace sitting on the edge of the bed smiling down at her. The short black dress she wore had ridden up her thighs, and her position revealed she wore nothing beneath.

'How are you feeling?' the woman asked.

'Numb, defeated,' Erica replied. 'Bitter and full of hate.'

'The microphones are off, you can talk freely,' Grace informed her. 'And you can trust me - this is off the record.'

Erica had learned the hard way to trust no one. 'Oh yeah, I've heard that one before,' she sneered.

'I didn't like what he did. Your stepfather. He went too far.'

'Why should you care?' Erica felt like crying at the reminder.

'How much do you know about me?' Grace asked her.

'Nothing,' Erica admitted frankly. 'Only what I've seen here.'

'I live in my own house, in the grounds,' Grace disclosed. 'I'm employed by *The Complex* to run things. And I'm very well paid, too.'

Erica wondered why she was being entrusted with such information. 'Why are you telling me all this?' she asked suspiciously. 'You've been as cruel to me as any of the Masters or Mistresses, so why the friendly act now?'

'I won't deny I get a huge buzz from domination, much more than I'm able to experience here,' Grace went on. 'Yes, I'm a cruel bitch, and I love using the whip and all the other equipment at our disposal here. That's why I jumped when they offered me the opportunity, when the place was originally set up. But being the senior housemistress here has its downside, too. I never seem able to relax and really indulge *myself*, not properly.'

'Is this leading somewhere?' Erica asked indifferently.

'Yes, it is,' Grace said decisively. 'I've a mind to have you as my personal slave.'

Erica was dumbstruck. 'And you're seeking my agreement?'

'I don't need your agreement. Officially you have no say in the deal. But I do want your oath of loyalty.'

'And you'd trust any oath I made to you?' Erica said, somewhat shocked and bemused by the disclosure. 'Why would you?' She tried to shift to a more comfortable position, her arms tingling.

'Here, let me untie you,' Grace offered, reaching for the ropes at her wrists and pulling at the knots until Erica's arms were free. 'You can do your own legs.'

Erica took some time rubbing the circulation back into her wrists and biceps before she unfastened her legs and feet, while Grace continued talking.

'Something about you has always fascinated me,' she went on. 'I don't know what it is, but there's something there; a spark that excites me. I think about you all the time; during the day when I'm working, and during the night when I'm... I want you, 51, all for myself.'

'You're a lesbian?' Erica asked.

'A bit of everything is what I am,' Grace answered openly. 'I've had relationships with men and women, but none of them came close to what I feel for you.'

'Just what exactly are you saying here?' Erica felt flushed and confused, barely able to believe what she was hearing.

'I think I'm in love with you.'

The candidness of the short sentence stunned Erica.

'You're what?' she gasped.

'That's why I want your loyalty. I'm hoping you can learn to return my love one day. I could have you to myself anyway; I've spoken to the other controllers and it's all set up. But I want your acquiescence first. I want you to want to be with me too.'

'I...' Erica was eager to agree; anything had to be better than living here and there was surely more chance she could escape at some point, but Grace stopped her.

'Before you say anything, I know what you're thinking,' she said. 'Don't imagine any freedom goes with this. I'll punish you daily and you'll be chained and bound just as you are here. I entertain guests a lot and you'll be used by them too, men and women. Just because I love you doesn't mean I'll be lenient with you. Possibly because I love you I'll be even harder, I'll test your loyalty whenever I can.'

Erica still wanted to take the chance. She had been in *The Complex* long enough to know there was no possibility of escape - but this would perhaps at least present her with an opportunity at some point. Surely Grace on her own could not be totally vigilant at all times.

'Very well,' she said, taking a deep breath, 'you have my loyalty, Mistress. Test it now, any way you want to.'

'I intend to,' Grace smiled back. 'Go and fetch a selection of implements from the cupboard. Things you particularly dislike.'

As Erica walked to the cupboard, aware her choice had to be right or this opportunity could disappear, Grace unzipped her dress and slid out of it. Erica returned with a cat, a cane and a crop, all of which had caused her considerable pain in the past.

'Put them on the bed,' Grace instructed, then sat beside them and spread her legs wide. 'Kneel, my slave. Kneel and pay homage to your Mistress.'

Erica sank to her knees and leaned forward to press her lips between Grace's thighs. She had done this for Grace many times before, but had never known her so wet, nor so responsive to her tongue's darting caress. However after a few minutes Grace pushed her head away and stood up.

'Go to the door, 51,' she said.

Puzzled, Erica stood and obeyed, and when she reached the portal she realised it was very slightly ajar.

'Open it,' Grace went on, and as the door swung wide Erica saw the usual morning business going on in the corridors beyond.

'Now push it to again. Don't close it completely or it'll lock itself, then come back here.'

Erica was more puzzled than ever. Grace climbed on the bed and lay face down, settling her cheek on the pillow and closing her eyes before stretching her arms towards the headboard. Her voice was gentle and relaxed. 'Tie my hands to the bed frame, my slave,' she said.

'But Mistress, I don't understand,' Erica said.

'Do as I tell you, 51. Tie them tight so I can't escape.'

'Are you a submissive too?' Erica asked.

Grace's eyes opened to look at her. 'No, I never have been and I never will be. Nor do I like receiving pain or humiliation. Now do as you're told.'

Erica shrugged and climbed onto the bed, wrapping one of the ropes that had secured her all night a few times around Grace's right wrist before tying it to the frame, then she quickly repeated the operation with her left wrist.

Grace sounded almost sleepy. 'Push a pillow under my hips and tie my feet as well.'

Erica glanced nervously towards the ceiling. Was this some horrible trap?

'Don't worry, there are no cameras on, nobody's watching or listening,' Grace said, as though reading her thoughts.

The pillow had the effect of raising Grace's bottom off the mattress, a perfect target for anyone of a mind to use it. Erica took the two remaining ropes and secured Grace's ankles to the foot of the bed, spread wide and making her totally accessible. Then she stood, not knowing what to do next.

'Um, what now, Mistress?' she asked tentatively.

'Have I ever been cruel to you, 51?' Grace suddenly asked.

'Yes, Mistress,' Erica replied honestly, 'very.'

'Often?'

'Yes, Mistress, often.'

'Well, here's your chance for revenge. Anything you want to do, go ahead. I can't stop you and you have my word there'll be no comeback. I won't hold anything against you. Make it good, though, because this will be your one and only chance, a never-to-be-repeated offer.'

'I...'

'Or you could make a bid for freedom,' Grace continued. 'The door is open. My dress is there, so are my shoes. Maybe, if you have enough nerve, you could make it. Nothing is set up here. Nobody is aware you might try, but nor are they primed to let you succeed. You'll just have to take your chances. But before you say another word, get a ball-gag and put it on me. That way I can't call out to alert someone. Do it now.'

Erica knew all too well where the ball-gags were kept, so she chose a large red one, pushed it into Grace's mouth and tightly buckled the strap at the back of her head. As an extra touch she reached for the blindfold still lying on the bed and fitted that too. Grace settled down into the softness of the mattress and the pillow beneath her hips, and waited.

Erica had some decisions to make. Cautiously she picked up Grace's dress and slipped it on, zipping it up. Should she make a run for it? She had tried it once before and failed, but she knew so much more about the place now. Her chances of escape were probably still pretty slim, but if she could defy the odds and get away she could fulfil the revenge she craved. She did not care what happened to her after that - they could lock her away forever if they wanted to. But the tantalising prospect of making her stepfather pay for what he had done to her made the huge risk she was considering very, very tempting.

But then, what about Grace? Could Erica afford the time to take revenge on her too, as the woman was tempting her to do? She feared it was a set-up that would surely end in her suffering, but since Grace was now unable to call out or raise the alarm Erica could use the very same implements that had been used so many times on her. Erica was feeling very bitter, still smarting as she was from her stepfather's betrayal.

She always found the cane to be the worst, so she picked it up in her right hand, moving to the side of the bed from where she could strike.

One thing worried her, though. Why should Grace do this? Why invite pain and humiliation when she had just admitted she hated both? And could it be that the sadistic woman really was in love with her? She even wondered if Grace was the only person to have loved her in her whole adult life, since her grandmother died all those years ago. Her stepfather certainly did not, he'd proved that, and how could her mother allow what had happened if she loved her? Tears welled in

Erica's eyes as she placed the cane back on the bed and moved towards the door. As she reached the heavy portal, saw again the light showing through the narrow gap where it was still open, she stood still and stared at it, her barrier for so long.

Erica reached forward and ran her hand gently across the smooth surface.

'Damn you,' she whispered to herself as she put her hand flat and pushed it firmly closed.

Walking back towards the bed she unzipped the dress and let it fall to the floor before she climbed on the bed and pressed her lips to one of Grace's smooth, naked shoulders.

'I accept your ownership, my Mistress,' she whispered. 'I am your property. May I make love to you before I untie you?'

Grace lifted her cheek from the pillow and slowly nodded. Erica knew it was only the rubber ball that stopped her smiling, but she did not want to remove it yet. She settled down on top of Grace, pressing the length of her body into the woman's naked back and resting her head between her shoulders. She was content to stay there for a while, enjoying, for once, tender contact without any of the cruelty that had become the norm.

Erica kissed her neck, ear and cheek, and then traced butterfly kisses up and down her Mistress's spine, dipping into the valley between her buttocks in a gesture of total surrender.

'You are my Mistress,' Erica breathed, and the realisation hit her that even though it was Grace who was physically helpless, it was still her who was being submissive. She let her hand seek down between Grace's cheeks until she felt warm dampness and the excited bud of her clitoris. She wanted to suckle it, but could not in this position, so in a sudden burst of need she was scrabbling at the bonds holding Grace to the bed, unfastening them sufficiently to let one wrist free, pulling off the blindfold and leaving Grace to unfasten her other arm while Erica started at her ankles. Both sensed each other's needs and worked rapidly, almost clumsily in their desire to have each other. When Grace was untied she unfastened her gag and dropped it to the floor.

'Tell me what to do, Mistress, please,' Erica begged.

'Just make love to me,' Grace coaxed. 'No whips, no ropes. Not this time.'

Erica pressed down to her again, their lips melting together in a passionate, deep, hungry kiss, their tongues searching each other's and their breasts moulding together. They rolled, not caring who was on top, and ending in a head to toe '69' position on their sides, their upper thighs raised to allow each other full oral access. Erica needed this - after her stepfather she needed honest love, honest lust; she just prayed she was not being played for a fool again, and for the second time in two days she was about to reach a real, shattering climax...

Afterwards the languid pair collapsed back on the bed, exhausted, and Grace giggled lightly.

Erica slid to the carpet beside the bed, still feeling submissive on her knees. Grace swung her legs off the bed and sat facing her. 'Good, 51. I'm glad you didn't see that as weakness on my part.'

'No, Mistress, not at all,' Erica said. 'But may I ask a question, please?'

Grace smiled again. 'You can ask.'

'Will the rules be the same as here?'

Grace thought for a few moments. 'Not quite, 51. You'll obey the same rules in terms of requests to speak and complete obedience, but your obedience, from this point forward, will be to me alone. Do you understand?'

'Yes, Mistress, I do,' Erica replied clearly.

'That does not mean other people won't use you, but you will only obey them if I alone have instructed it. I warn you, though, that any attempt to escape or disobey in any way will see you brought right back here immediately. I happen to know that one of our Middle Eastern guests was about to buy you, and I don't recommend that at all.'

Erica shuddered. She had heard rumours of slaves being taken overseas to situations that made *The Complex* seem like a holiday camp, and she definitely did not want to find out if they were true. 'Thank you, Mistress,' she said, with growing sincerity.

'For what?'

'For buying me. For showing me some love.'

'Just don't imagine it will buy you any favours, 51.'

'No, Mistress.'

'I think a measure of proof of your devotion is needed. Lean over the bed, and remain still.'

Erica did as she was told, resting her breasts and face on the cool bedcovers while Grace stood and picked up the cane. Taking a position behind her new possession she struck hard and swiftly, six times in all, while Erica cried out with each powerful stroke.

'And one other thing,' Grace said as she placed the cane back on the bed. 'I don't want to be thanked for administering a punishment like so many of the others do. If you're grateful after I've punished you, it means I've not punished you enough and I'll do it harder the next time. I expect honesty from you at all times. If I hurt you cry, scream, beg me to stop. If I amuse you, laugh. I want honesty, remember?'

Erica nodded meekly. 'Yes, Mistress.'

'Good. Anything you want to add, while you are permitted?'

Erica nodded again. 'Yes please, Mistress.'

'What is it?'

'That really hurt.' Erica managed a rueful smile through her tears, and Grace smiled back, reached for her dress and started to put it on.

'OK, wait here,' she said. 'You don't need to do anything; it's all arranged. You'll be packed up and delivered, as is the tradition. Do you have any questions?'

'If I may, Mistress?' Erica dared. 'Can I say goodbye to 83 before I go?'

Grace looked her up and down. 'No, you cannot. Firstly, it's not permitted, and secondly, 83 has been bought already; by your disappointed Middle Eastern gentleman. She's being packed for shipment as we speak. You'll not see her again. Now get some rest; they'll come for you in less than an hour.' Grace slipped her shoes on and knocked on the heavy door, which quickly clicked open. She glanced back at Erica for a moment before she left.

Erica felt euphoric to be leaving such an odious place, but also felt a tinge of sadness. She had a few friends here, bound by their mutual desperation and suffering, and she guessed she would never see any of them ever again. She lay on her bed for the last time and closed her eyes, wondering what the future would hold, particularly fearful for Beth.

CHAPTER 14

Erica had never seen what happened to slaves when they were bought, though she'd heard rumours. She had no idea whether her treatment was usual, either. Three men arrived at her door noisily, one telling her to stand while the other two wheeled in a trolley on top of which was what looked like a coffin. Maybe that's how the girls were transported without anyone noticing, in a coffin in a hearse. She thought it was stupid considering Grace had said her house was in the grounds, but the controllers did like to adhere to their rituals.

The man who had spoken lifted the lid of the padded box while the other two men picked her up and lifted her into it. The cream-coloured satin was cool on her skin as she settled in, the padding moulding itself comfortably around her shape. A strap was fitted across her forehead and tightened, and then another around her neck, with one at her waist, across each thigh, knee, ankle, elbow and wrist, until no movement was possible at all. What looked like a combination of a breathing mask and a ball-gag was pushed into her mouth and fastened over her nose, the pipe leading to some sort of hidden vent in the top of the box. Erica fought back the mounting panic as the lid was closed and heavy clasps fastened noisily in place. In her padded darkness she heard voices, but could not work out what they were saying.

She became aware that she was moving, that the wheels on the trolley were crossing her doorway and travelling along the carpeted corridors towards the main entrance. She tried to imagine where she was and almost wished she could have gained the satisfaction of seeing those rooms for the very last time.

The movement stopped suddenly and she was being carried. She imagined being taken down the steps to the gravel drive where the car would be waiting. She thought she heard the car's door being closed and she certainly felt it start to move. It travelled for perhaps ten minutes before she felt it stop, and soon she was being carried again, up steps, judging from the angle, and into her new home. Her new prison.

She felt herself being placed on something solid and unmoving, and waited for the lid to open; yet nothing happened. Nothing. Silence. No motion. She was alone, she was sure of that. Another test, maybe. Whatever it was she could do nothing but wait, and sleep maybe; despite her confinement she felt unusually relaxed.

She had no idea of how long she slept, but when she awoke she was immediately hungry. The clasps on the box were being unfastened one by one. The light hurt her eyes when the lid opened and she clenched them shut against it.

'Welcome to your new home,' Grace said. 'Take your time getting used to the light, and I'll be back in a minute.'

Erica gradually opened her eyes. The ceiling above her was a lot more classical than the modern sterility of *The Complex*, with ornate covings and a classic chandelier almost directly above her. She could not see any more of her new surroundings, but the light filling it looked natural. If this was to be her room was it possible she would actually have a window to gaze out of, and be able to tell when it was day or night? After years with a windowless room the thought filled her with the kind of excitement a child would have at Christmas.

When Grace returned a few minutes later she was talking to a man whom Erica could not see, but was sure she recognised his nervous voice. Her mind tried to match it to memories, and all too soon she remembered - he was the man who had welded her nipple rings in place. She felt cold fear inside, wondering what torture could require his presence again.

'I bought you a present,' Grace told her, as if in answer. She was holding a velvet box, which she opened and tilted forward so that Erica could see its contents. Inside was a heavy gold collar, with small eyelets attached at the front and the sides. 'I had it made especially for you. It's solid gold, and engraved. It says, "51, property of Grace Roberts".'

Erica's eyes must have reflected her question: how had Grace known she would agree to being her new slave, or did it matter? Grace reached down and removed the breathing apparatus from Erica's face.

'Ask your question, 51,' she permitted.

'How did you know I would succumb to you, Mistress?' she said, her voice a little timid. 'Or didn't it matter?'

'Yes, it mattered. I'd have probably bought you anyway, but it mattered. I'd not have given you this unless you'd agreed. I can force you to do anything, you know that, but that doesn't mean you've surrendered, only that you've been compelled. This signifies your willing acquiescence and that turns me on immensely. So will you wear my collar, 51, permanently?'

Erica opened her mouth to answer, but Grace laid a finger across her lips. 'One other thing you should see before you respond,' she said quietly, then lifted the collar from the box and tilted it so that Erica could see some additional engraving on the inside. 'This can't be seen at *The Complex*, but you and I will know it's there.' She held the collar forward so Erica could read the inscription. 'Erica, property of Grace,' she read to the bound girl.

The fact that Grace had used her real name touched Erica deeply. At long last someone was treating her as a person, not just a number. Her emotions welled up inside. 'Yes, I'll wear your collar, Mistress,' she said. 'I'll be your willing property. Thank you.'

'And it's our secret, remember? Nobody must know about the inscription. Agreed?'

Erica nodded, so Grace smiled and unfastened the straps holding her in the box. Erica sat while the timid man readied his equipment. This time she knew what the grubby looking cloth was for, but this time he took longer and asked for Grace's help holding the clamps. She insisted on encircling Erica's throat with the gold band, looking deep into her eyes and smiling as she closed it. The collar had a fitting that slid together but was not intended as a locking clasp. Like her nipple rings, once this was fitted it would need a cutter to remove it.

The man slid the cloth under it, using a long pair of pliers to hold it away from Erica's skin while he busied himself with the blowtorch. Erica turned her head away from the heat as he worked, and less than five minutes later she heard the hiss as he used cold water to cool the weld. A few more minutes with a small battery-powered polisher and he stood back to let Grace see the finished article.

Grace looked, reaching to adjust its position. She held a mirror so Erica could see the apparently seamless gold circle - a sign of her slavery, yet somehow comfortable and safe.

'Welcome to my house, my slave,' Grace smiled.

'Thank you, Mistress,' Erica replied, instinctively dipping her head slightly.

The man quickly packed up his tools and left, and Erica looked around her room. Immaculate wallpaper gave way to sumptuous deep-pile carpets and a pink ceiling above. The heavy-draped windows looked out over lush green pastureland sloping away to trees, behind which she could just see the roof of *The Complex*, a chilling reminder if ever she needed one.

Grace sat next to her on the bed. 'For tonight only, so don't think this is any relaxation of the rules, you may ask questions freely. For tonight, as a special welcome as my property, I will call you Erica. And before you ask, no, you may not call me Grace, understood?'

'Yes, Mistress.'

'The windows are alarmed and will not open far enough for you to get out. All exterior doors have combination locks. Escape, if you did try, wouldn't be easy; and there are the dogs, traps and fences to get through too.'

'I won't try and escape, Mistress,' Erica stated firmly.

Grace looked at her curiously, hoping she could have faith in that.

'Right, let me take you on a tour of the house,' she eventually said. 'But before we do I intend to indulge myself.'

She stood and walked over to a chest of drawers positioned against one wall, taking out some fine gold chains and cuffs. She had Erica stand while she fixed the cuffs on her wrists and used small padlocks to lock them there, attaching the ends of two of the chains as she snapped them shut. From her wrists the chains were threaded through her nipple rings and fastened by two more padlocks to the two eyelets each side of her collar, Grace pulling them tight so that Erica's hands were held in front of her breasts as she stood there. Grace picked up the third chain and locked it to the front eyelet, wrapping the loose end round her hand a few times before pulling Erica into an intense kiss that left her quite breathless.

The décor throughout the house was similar to Erica's bedroom; ornate mouldings and pastel wallpapers, such a contrast to the sterile blandness of *The Complex* such a short distance away. Grace's hand was always there to guide Erica up and down stairs, making sure that the inability to use her hands did not cause an accident.

Grace's own bedroom was total luxury, dominated by a large circular bed big enough to accommodate an orgy. Grace showed her that under the valance were set numerous metal rings around the periphery, easily utilised to secure a willing or unwilling slave. Grace's own bathroom had a sunken spa bath set in the centre.

On a sudden whim Grace attacked Erica's breasts with her hands and mouth, a task made harder by her chained hands, but Grace did not falter, suckling her nipples around the gold rings and gradually pulling Erica to the floor, where she pushed her legs apart and kissed her way between them, producing in Erica the tenderest, sexiest feelings she'd had for such a long time. She was quickly brought to the brink of an explosive orgasm, and held there for some minutes until Grace took her over the top, licking, biting and sucking at her clitoris and labia.

'I'll take you whenever I want you,' she growled through a mouthful of wet female flesh.

Eventually they made their way to the lounge, its Georgian windows overlooking the rolling landscape, and Erica was surprised to see a man sitting on one of the settees.

'This is my brother, Jonathon,' Grace offered by way of introduction.

The man turned slowly to face them. He looked slightly older than Grace, but there was a definite family resemblance. 'Come over here,' he growled.

Erica was so used to obeying anyone for fear of punishment that she was just about to move to him, but she remembered Grace's words and stopped, glancing at her.

'I said come here, bitch,' Jonathon repeated.

Again Erica glanced at Grace, and finally the woman smiled slightly and nodded. Erica moved quickly to the sofa and stood in front of the man, looking down, not meeting his piercing gaze.

'Why did you not obey immediately, bitch?' he asked her. 'My sister claims you're a good slave.'

Again he met silence. Erica sensed she was being tested.

'Tell her to obey me, Grace,' he snapped angrily.

'Patience, brother, patience,' Grace smiled as she moved forward to sit on the other settee. '51, tell him why you didn't obey.'

'I'm sorry, Master,' Erica said sheepishly, 'but my Mistress said to obey only her unless she tells me to obey someone else. I apologise if I displeased you.'

'I want to have her, Grace.' His tone and demeanour were blunt, uncompromising.

'I should explain, 51, that my brother is a soldier. He's been stationed in the Falklands for several months. He got home yesterday and he's not had a female for a long time, so I decided to let him use and have you. Any objections?'

Erica swallowed hard. The recent bonding with Grace had lulled her into a feeling of cosy security, as if Grace was now her loving protector. Yet here she was offering her to a man who looked every bit as brutal as the normal guests at *The Complex* but with the added urgency of someone desperate to have her. 'No, Mistress,' she said tentatively, 'whatever you say.'

'How do you want her?' Grace turned to her brother.

'Without those chains for a start. I want to get at those tits.'

'Do you want her tied down?' Grace spoke coolly, almost as if Erica was not in the room.

'Sounds nice,' Jonathon drooled.

'How about I warm her up first?' Grace continued.

'Meaning what?'

'Come with me, I'll show you,' Grace said, standing and taking hold of Erica's leash. She led the way out of the room and turned left along the hallway, until she reached a door that led down carpeted stairs to a basement, furnished to the same standards as the rest of the house, making the assembly of racks and beams and instruments of bondage and punishment even more incongruous. She pulled Erica to the centre of the room and walked round to face her. Jonathon closed the door and sat in an armchair. 'Do you believe I love you, 51?' the woman asked.

Erica nodded. 'Yes, Mistress, I do.'

'This will be to prove it to you, but afterwards I'll want to know if you still believe me. Until then, I don't want to hear a word from you.'

Erica stood still and silent while Grace unfastened her wrists and breasts and took her to a leather bench by one wall. Pushing her face down over it, on her knees, sprawled forward, Grace secured her hands to leather cuffs at the top edge. Another strap over her waist pinned Erica's body in place, and finally Grace buckled two straps to hold her knees secure.

'What do you think?' Grace asked him.

'Nice arse,' was the best he could come up with. Erica did not like Jonathon at all, but maybe that was their intention.

'What do you do to her?' he asked. 'Normally, I mean?'

'Anything I want,' Grace said casually. 'Anything at all. I like to beat her. Do you want me to demonstrate?'

'Why not?' He settled deeper in his chair, ready for the show.

'Yes,' Grace repeated casually, 'why not?'

Erica waited, not quite sure of what she would be beaten with, how hard or for how long. All she was sure of was that it would happen and she could not prevent it. Some of the slaves at *The Complex* said they had got used to the beatings, but Erica never had. Each time hurt just as much as the previous one. She had a feeling this was likely to be intense, since Grace was obviously out to make a point.

The first stroke took her by complete surprise, since there was no warning at all. She jerked her head up instinctively from the force of the blow, wailing out her agony. Grace took no notice, laying on the next stroke and the next with painful rapidity until Erica's bottom was on fire. Erica was sobbing and exhausted by the tenth stroke, when Grace paused.

'Do you want me to stop, 51?' she asked. 'Be honest with me. I won't tolerate dishonesty.'

'Y-yes, Mistress, I want you to stop,' Erica whimpered.

'And you know I won't, don't you? What if I told you that if you said you *didn't* want me to stop, then I would, what then? Do you want me to stop, 51?'

'Yes, Mistress,' she repeated.

'Even though your honesty means I'll carry on?'

'Yes, Mistress. I won't lie to you.'

'Very well, my slave.'

Grace did not say another word until she had applied another ten strokes, as hard as the previous ten and delivered without pause or mercy.

'That's it, enough now,' she said at last.

'Can I do it too?' her brother asked immediately.

'No, Jonathon, you cannot. She's mine, not yours.'

'But you said...' He was openly disappointed.

'You can have her in any way I say, dear brother. She won't object. Any other way and she'll refuse you.'

'Her arse is bright red,' he mused. 'You did a good job on that.'

'So have that,' Grace said simplistically. 'Use it. Fuck it.'

'OK, I will,' he agreed eagerly. 'But preferably without you watching, little sis.'

'Very well. I've no wish to watch you buggering my beautiful new slave. You can use her rectum, but that's it, OK?'

'Yes, if you say, though how you'll know...' His lascivious leer scared Erica.

'I'll know,' Grace insisted confidently, 'because she'll tell me. 51...'

'Yes, Mistress?'

'If he does anything over and above what I've stipulated I want you to scream for me. Understood?'

'Understood, Mistress,' Erica said gratefully.

'And you'll use plenty of this,' Grace continued, taking a tube of KY from a cupboard. 'Actually, I'll do it, just to be sure.'

She bent behind Erica and squeezed a generous portion between the bound girl's cheeks. The cold against her stinging skin made her start, but it soon warmed up as Grace's hand smoothed it between them. She crooked two of her fingers together and, aided by the KY, slid them into Erica's rosebud, sliding in until she could go no further, twisting her fingers round to spread the lubricant. Then the fingers were gone, leaving Erica with a strange feeling of loss.

'Right, you've got half an hour,' she told him. 'If you can last that long,' she smirked.

'I'll last that long,' he replied cockily.

'Well, we'll see,' she said as she swept up out of the basement room.

Erica waited, unable to see what he was doing behind her, but aware of the rustling of his clothes as he undressed, and before long she felt him behind her.

'Right,' he started, 'my sis says I can have your arse, so I will. Brace yourself.'

Erica felt his erection nudge between her legs, searching for its way into her secret passage. Steadying himself with one hand on the small of her back he pressed forward until he gained entry, and when he was sure her tight ring of muscle had yielded, he lunged hard.

'Aaaagh!' Erica gasped as he sank inside her to the hilt.

'Too big for you, huh?' he sniggered through gritted teeth.

Erica decided there was no way to win by saying anything, so she remained silent as Jonathon rutted in and out of her tight rear passage, grunting about just how good he was and how big his cock was. Erica loathed the man and decided to accelerate things, clenching her sphincter until she was squeezing him with each thrust.

'God, she was right!' he gasped. 'You are very... very... aaaagh!' And with that he quickly erupted inside her, within seconds his cock shrivelling and slipping wetly from between her bottom cheeks.

'Fuck,' he groaned, 'I wanted to enjoy some more of that.'

Erica smiled to herself.

'Whore!' he spat at her. 'You did that deliberately, didn't you? You made me come too soon!' He moved to her head and grabbed her hair, yanking her head back until she grimaced with the pain. 'Answer me! You did, didn't you?'

He was not allowing her much freedom to move, but she did manage to nod. After all, had Grace not forbidden her to talk?

'I'll fucking show you!' he spat at her, then was gone, returning a few seconds later carrying the same cane Grace had used.

'I'll show you,' he repeated, raising it high before bringing it down hard across her back.

Erica screamed, shouting for her Mistress, glad to be able to obey her, and Grace was there in seconds.

'I told you, Jonathon,' she seethed. 'I warned you about abusing my slave without my permission!'

'The bitch tricked me,' he yelled at her, raising the cane again.

'Put it down, *now!*' Grace told him, her tone cold and unyielding. 'Then get out of here and don't come back!'

'But...'

'Get out,' she repeated coldly.

Jonathon growled, walked to his clothes and picked them up.

'You can dress upstairs,' she told him uncompromisingly, and then repeated, 'Don't come back. My debt to you is paid. We're even now.'

Already she was ignoring him, moving to the cupboard to fetch a tube of cream, but this time one to salve Erica's bottom, and the angry welt across her back. When she had smoothed some of the cream in and it started to take effect, she unfastened Erica's bonds and took her to the comfortable settee.

'I need to be cruel to you, Erica,' she said quietly. 'And I'm not sorry for that.'

'I know, Mistress. I accept that.'

Grace kissed her hard on the lips. 'I hope you'll be happy here,' she smiled.

'I hope *we'll* be happy, Mistress,' Erica corrected her.

Grace smiled, a little wearily. 'There's something I want you to tell me, Erica, and I want your honest answer.'

Erica sat and waited, wondering what this could be.

'Is there anything, anything at all, which would make you try and escape from here, from me?' Grace asked.

Erica did not need to think for very long. 'One thing only, Mistress,' she admitted.

'Which is?'

'The chance to get even with my stepfather.'

'Get even?' Grace echoed. 'What exactly do you mean by "get even"?'

'To kill him,' Erica said without hesitation.

Grace looked at her strangely, although clearly unfazed by the frank honesty of the response. 'But what about the consequences?'

Erica shrugged blithely. 'I don't care about any consequences.'

Grace thought for a few moments, her expression giving nothing away as she closely scrutinised the girl, staring deep into her eyes. 'Very well,' she finally said, as though making her mind up about something.

'Very well?' Erica echoed.

'What if I said I could fix things for you?' Grace said. 'I know people. I have contacts.'

'Y-you mean...?' Erica stammered, barely able to believe she had an ally at last.

Grace nodded and smiled reassuringly.

Erica let out a long breath, the enormity of what they were discussing making her pulse race. 'Well,' she ventured hesitantly, 'revenge is all that's kept me sane since he had me abducted. But why would you...?'

'I'll help you,' Grace said calmly. 'I'll arrange everything. But it'll have to be our secret. Afterwards you'll belong to me, utterly. You'll never be able to leave me. *Never.*'

'You don't have to blackmail me into loyalty, Mistress,' Erica told her.

'I know I don't, but I'm a ruthless bitch when I want something. Now what do you say? There'll be no going back. Revenge for a lifetime of slavery; you choose.'

Erica looked down at her hands for a few moments, then back up at Grace, decision made. 'Yes, Mistress,' she announced, 'I choose to be yours forever.'

CHAPTER 15

Erica had been dreaming, but the more she tried to remember the dream the more distant it became. She opened her eyes, half expecting to see Grace in the room, but she was alone.

She liked to have the curtains closed, since from her bedroom window she could see the hated *Complex* in the distance, a constant reminder that she could be sent back there if she transgressed, to the cruel masters and mistresses.

Erica was glad Grace had chosen to buy her. She could easily have been sold to someone overseas, someone far crueller than Grace. Not that Grace wasn't cruel; she was very keen on repeatedly demonstrating that she was in control and could do precisely what she liked. Erica had no choices, so she made love with her Mistress whenever commanded, or with whomever her Mistress chose for her.

A distant clatter told her there was someone in the house. She adjusted her position on the bed slightly, and the chains linking the locked leather cuffs to the ring at the left side of the bed-head rattled as she moved. She was restrained in some way every night, not to prevent her escape, but because Grace decided it - and to remind Erica that she was a piece of owned property.

Footsteps approached her door, and she recognised the sounds of her mistress easily.

'Good morning, my darling,' Grace smiled as she appeared in the doorway.

'Good morning, Mistress,' Erica replied as the woman approached the bed.

'On your front,' Grace told her, and as Erica moved awkwardly to lie face down Grace reached for the zip at the back of her black dress and drew it down. She then slipped the dress off her shoulders, revealing the narrow straps of her black bra and the well filled C-cups. She watched as the dress fell lower, until the equally inadequate thong came into view.

When the dress had gone Grace reached into the bedside cabinet and took out a crop. No reason was given to Erica for the fact she was about to be beaten, but nothing new there. Grace even smiled as she reached across and pulled the duvet towards Erica's feet, letting it slide to the floor at the foot of the bed.

'I've got an interesting conundrum for you,' Grace told her, running her fingertips across her slave number, 51, tattooed into her buttock. 'I've decided to forbid you to cry out when I beat you.'

Erica waited as Grace paused, wanting the second part of her announcement to have its full effect. 'You understand?' she asked.

'Yes... Mistress,' Erica said tentatively.

'The only problem, for you at least,' the woman added, 'is that I intend to beat you until you cry.' Grace paused again to let the message sink in. 'Do you have any questions?'

'So the only way to obey is to be silent?' Erica asked, uneasily.

'Correct.'

'But you keep going until I make a sound?'

'Right again.'

'May I ask the penalty for disobedience, Mistress?'

'I haven't decided yet. Let's be honest here; you won't cry out until you have to because you're a proud bitch and you want to show me you can take anything I can dish out. And I'll keep going because I need to break you. Right?'

Erica did not need to reply.

'But I will give you one get-out,' Grace offered. 'If you can take it until you pass out, I'll stop. But no pretending.'

'With respect, Mistress, I think you know me better than that.'

Grace smiled down at her slave, excited about the pain and punishment she was about to give. She knew Erica would not be broken easily, but that was the very thing that attracted her to the girl in the first place. 'Are you ready?' she asked.

'Does it make a difference?' Erica sighed, bracing herself.

'No, it doesn't.' Grace raised the crop ready to strike, before adding enigmatically, 'It's all set up. I have a party at the weekend, at which you will be the centre of attention, and when that's over, he's all yours. Does that please you?'

Erica's stomach tightened with a mixture of excitement and dread. 'Y-yes, Mistress... it does.'

'Good. So now you can show me how grateful you are...'

Grace swept the crop down hard against Erica's buttocks, before she had time to prepare herself. The merest gasp escaped her lips before she managed to control it. She had become accustomed to being beaten, even to the point where she could switch herself off to the pain doled out by the less experienced Masters and Mistresses who used her. One or two had been exhausted from their efforts because she had taken their cruelty without a murmur. She still did not understand why they needed to beat her, but that was irrelevant. They did it, and that's all that mattered.

But occasionally there would be one who delighted in her ability to withstand punishment. They would be determined to crack her, to prove there was no way she could win. Grace was one of those, and Erica knew it. She would cry out, sooner or later. But for now she could take it.

The blows rained down across her rear, scorching her buttocks, striping them. Grace was an expert, concentrating on specific areas, keeping the power down until Erica had become accustomed to it, then suddenly choosing a different area or a much more severe stroke.

It had become a game, where Erica would try and anticipate when and where Grace would strike and Grace watching every twitch of Erica's body, waiting for the moment when she could break through her pain barriers.

Erica could see Grace in the mirrors along the wall to her right, watching the way her eyes looked down at her, seeing the delighted concentration and the tensing of her features each time she was ready to strike. It gave Erica an edge in the anticipation game, for now at least.

'You're waiting, aren't you?' Grace asked, as if reading her thoughts. 'You're trying to anticipate when I'll switch strokes.'

'Yes, Mistress, I am.' There was little point in lying, but she knew what was next; she would have to close her eyes or turn away, or she would be blindfolded.

'Today that's OK,' Grace announced, surprising her. 'I want you to be able to anticipate. That way it won't be a sudden surprise that will make you scream, it'll be pure pain. So watch me, watch how I strike harder and harder until I make you cry, my love.'

And with that Grace stepped up a gear; not suddenly, but gradually increasing the power of her strokes until she was glistening with sweat from her efforts. Erica could see her tense each time she was about to strike, gritting her teeth to focus the power into the crop.

Each time it landed Erica clenched her teeth, but slowly and surely the pain was getting through; Grace was finding new sources of angst with uncanny accuracy, and the more Erica resisted crying out the more determined Grace became, and the more venom she put into it.

Erica had suffered something like thirty strokes when her mouth fell open to let a long, strangled gasp escape. It signalled to Grace that she was on the path now, to losing, to disobeying, to being broken. Each successively more vicious stroke repeated the gasping moan, with Erica pulling hard against her bonds, uncaring of how they cut into her wrists. She twisted to each side to try and ease the pain from the blows that Grace was now concentrating in the centre of her back.

'Stay still!' Grace barked, unwilling to take any disobedience now. Erica's back arched, trying desperately, hopelessly, to find some relief from the whipping. The moans and gasps flowed freely now and she knew she was lost. Yet still she held it, tensing to meet each stroke.

'Cry out,' Grace urged. 'Beg me to stop. You know you want to.'

'No!' Erica gasped defiantly, yet even as she refused she knew she was lost. Grace was giving no quarter.

Grace paused for a moment, just long enough to gather her strength for the final onslaught. She looked down at Erica, who stared back up at her. Both knew it was time; time which stretched into slow motion as Grace raised the crop high over her right shoulder, to hover there a moment, waiting for the instant of total capitulation.

Then she struck, hard, with the force of her arm amplified by the timing of the flick of the crop. The pain of the last ten or fifteen minutes was immaterial, simply a preparation for this moment.

The sound of the whip as it lashed into Erica's flesh was completely drowned out by her scream, and Grace, in her turn, joined in, celebrating the exhaustion of the job she had done. Erica's wails slowly turned to wracking sobs as Grace threw the crop aside, its job for the day completed. She sat on the bed next to her slave.

'You're a mess,' she eventually said. 'You should have given in earlier.'

'It-it's what you w-wanted,' Erica whimpered, sniffing away her tears. 'It's what I had to give, or what I had to have taken from me.'

'Are you my property, Erica?' the woman asked.

'Yes, Mistress, yours to use and abuse.' She tried to turn over, but the pain was far too intense and Grace told her to stay as she was.

'You do excite me, Erica,' Grace told her as she smoothed some salving lotion into her back.

'You excite me too, Mistress,' she replied openly.

'On your knees then, and suck me,' Grace instructed, reaching to unfasten the cuffs, then she sat on the side of Erica's bed while her slave sank stiffly to her knees on the floor, moving her hands to the thong.

'No, leave it on,' she was told as Grace spread her legs wide. 'Just pull it aside when you need to.'

Erica kissed slowly up the inside of Grace's left thigh, but Grace grabbed her hair and pulled her upwards. 'I don't need any foreplay,' she groaned impatiently. 'Just do me.'

Pulling aside the soaking material, Erica kissed and licked Grace's labia, flicking her tongue between and seeking out the hard bud of her clitoris. Grace had been right about not needing any foreplay; she was soaking. Erica lapped her eagerly.

Meanwhile Grace looked down at the bobbing head, wallowing in the sensations and looking beyond to the angry skin on Erica's back, bearing the marks of her complete domination. She put her hand behind Erica's neck and pulled her in, hard.

'Suck me, damn you,' she growled. 'Make me come.'

Erica knew her Mistress well, and her tongue soon had Grace gasping on the edge, where she kept her teetering for a few minutes. Dipping a straightened finger deep into her own pussy she coated it in the lubrication she wanted, and when she speared it deep into Grace's anus, flicking her tongue across her bud with greater intensity and focus, Grace exploded into a crashing, exhausting, exhilarating climax.

Erica hung on as Grace bucked her hips, and then kissed gently between the woman's pussy lips as she subsided, stroking her slave's hair and trying to steady her breathing.

'Just because... just because you do that so well doesn't mean I regret beating you,' Grace purred languidly.

'I know, Mistress.'

'And it won't make me any more lenient next time.'

'I know that too, Mistress.'

'You're a good slave, Erica. I love beating you.'

'May I ask a question, Mistress?'

'You can ask.'

Erica had often thought about this, but had never found an answer. 'Why do you love beating me?'

'Because I can, Erica,' Grace answered. 'Because I have all the power, all the control, and you have none. I don't expect you to understand, merely to endure.'

'Yes, Mistress.' She was right; Erica still did not understand.

'Now, go and have a cool shower and I'll put some lotion on your back. Then I want to tell you about my party.'

CHAPTER 16

By the weekend Erica's marks had all but faded. Grace was keen that her guests would be able to see the evidence of the punishment on her slave's back, but equally keen that any discomfort from them had eased, leaving Erica able to be whipped and punished afresh, for their entertainment.

Erica was almost looking forward to the party; after all, she had been promised that when it was over she would be able to get her long-awaited revenge.

Grace had no regular men friends, not in the sense of a stable relationship, at any rate. She had told Erica that she preferred women, but had no objection to an occasional dalliance with a man, including, if she was in the mood, lots of wild, abandoned sex. She did have a distinct urge to prove herself in the company of men though, and showing off her power over her beautiful slave would be a good way of doing so.

Erica watched the caterers from *The Complex* arrive during the day with their platters of food, setting it all out in Grace's large dining room. Erica did not flinch at what two men were assembling. She had seen similar contraptions in *The Complex*, though she had never been in one. They referred to them as *frames*. Completely constructed from strong tubular steel, the movable parts could be adjusted and clamped in position so that her head, legs and arms could be fixed in any pose required. The whole frame was attached by a universal joint to a heavy stand, in such a way that the whole could be rotated, swivelled and tilted. They would be able to put her into any position. She tried to imagine what she would look like to the party guests. A thick rubber sheet had been placed under the stand to protect the carpet, but from what? She did not want to think about that at all.

When they left the room Erica examined the thick leather straps that would hold her in the contraption, and she didn't hear Grace come into the room behind her. 'What do you think of it?' The sound of her voice made Erica start.

'Does it matter?'

'Not really, but I want to know. Does it excite you? Does it scare you?'

'It doesn't excite me, Mistress,' Erica admitted. 'I hope that doesn't disappoint you.'

'Far from it. I don't want it to excite you. I want you to dislike it. I want you to know you're suffering because I own you.'

'Yes, Mistress.' It still amazed Erica, even after all her time at *The Complex*, that anyone could think they owned another human being. Yet she knew it was the truth.

'May I ask...?' Erica's voice trailed off, wishing she had not started.

'What? Speak.'

'It's nothing, Mistress, sorry.'

'Tell me or get whipped right now.'

'Will I be beaten tonight?'

'Yes.'

'By you?'

'By me and by anyone else who wants to beat you. I have a rather special treat for our guests. Do you want me to tell you what it is?'

'As you please, Mistress—' Erica never saw the slap coming, but it hit her with so much force it sent her staggering back so she had to grab the frame for support.

'When I ask you a question, 51, it means I want a definite answer.'

'Yes, Mistress,' Erica sobbed meekly. 'Please, I'd like to know.'

'I want to see you defiled in the most spectacular way. I want them to come all over you until it's pouring off your face and body, matting your hair and choking your throat. I've got fifteen men coming, some with their partners and some alone, and I've told them what I want. I've got some slaves being sent over from *The Complex* to help out. I anticipate each man should be able to come at least twice and every last drop will be spent on you or in you. Does that disgust you?'

Erica nodded honestly. 'Yes, Mistress.'

'Good.' Grace retrieved a key from the chain about her neck and started to unlock Erica's cuffs. 'Now go and shower. Clean your teeth, wash your hair and make up faultlessly. Wear the clothes I've put out for you. Come down here when you're ready. You have two hours, so that should be enough. From this moment forward you will not speak unless told to do so. And I warn you, 51, if you fail to please any of my guests I will make you pass out when I next whip you. Understand?'

Erica nodded.

'Go on then.'

Erica stepped out of the shower and wrapped herself in a large bath towel while she dried and brushed her hair until it bounced with its own natural waves, shining in the dressing-table lights. She let the towel slip to the floor while she applied her makeup and renewed the red varnish on her finger and toenails.

Only when she was happy with her appearance did she turn her attention to the clothes on her bed. No surprises there: a long black dress, the skirt slashed up the centre almost to her waist so as to reveal her legs as she walked. The top was nothing more than a halter strap emerging from the waistband, ready to be fastened behind her neck and ready to reveal most of her breasts - all that would be covered were two-inch wide strips over her nipples and the gold rings fitted permanently to the pierced holes therein.

Unsurprisingly no bra had been placed on the bed, and as the dress offered no support Erica was glad her breasts were pert and firm. She fastened the wispy black suspender belt around her waist and unfolded the black seamed stockings, making sure she didn't snag them with her nails. She sat on her bed to roll on her stockings and fasten the suspenders, and then stood to step into the impossibly small thong.

Erica caught sight of herself in the mirror. If anything the years at *The Complex* had made her even more attractive, enforced fitness and healthy diet taking away all traces of the slight puppy-fat she'd had when she was first abducted. She knew she looked good, but the sight did not please her. She should be using her attractiveness on men whom she could pick and choose, not on any person wealthy or powerful enough to have her regardless of her wishes.

With a sigh Erica reached for the dress and stepped into it before fastening the halter behind her neck. Eyeing her reflection in the mirror she adjusted the halter straps across her breasts, noticing how the rings in her nipples, and for that matter her nipples too, pressed out against the black satin.

She stepped into the black high-heeled shoes and walked out onto the plush burgundy carpet of the landing to descend the stairs.

In the lounge Grace turned to face Erica as she entered. Behind her stood two men in dinner suits, accompanied by attractive blondes in identically-styled dresses, one in light blue and the other deep red, each cut low to reveal the upper slopes of tanned breasts, the hemlines only reaching halfway down equally tanned thighs. Erica realised they were twins before she took in the appearance of the men, who stood tall and athletic, with dark-brown hair greying slightly at the temples. With some surprise Erica guessed they, too, were twins. She also noticed that all five faces were now turned her way, registering her surprise.

'Is this the one?' one of the men asked, his eyes not averting from his appraisal of Erica.

'Yes, this is my slave, known only as 51,' Grace responded. 'She's available for anything you demand of her.'

'Anything?' the man asked, one eyebrow slightly raised.

Grace nodded confidently. 'Anything.'

'On your knees then, slave,' he said to Erica, his voice quiet yet commanding.

Erica did not hesitate; she knew better than to do so. She sank to her knees on the carpet and waited as the man left his companions and walked over to her. Grabbing her hair he roughly yanked her head back to push his fingers between her lips and examine her teeth. This was a new one on Erica, despite all she had been through.

His hands moved on, downwards, possessive, across her breasts, taking the halter straps as they went, drawing them aside so her breasts sprang forth, ready to be cupped and mauled.

'Nice,' he breathed. 'I like the rings. One could lead her round on a leash with them.'

114

'Be my guest,' Grace told him, already moving to the ubiquitous cabinet full of her instruments of subjugation. She took out two dog leads, moving quickly across to the man and holding them out.

'Later,' he smiled. 'Maybe later.'

Meanwhile Erica noticed one of the girls move to the cabinet, examining the contents. 'Kinky,' she mused, removing a pair of silver handcuffs, then a second. She joined her partner with Erica, reaching behind to fasten Erica's wrists behind her back with one pair of cuffs. She then leaned forward and kissed Erica full on the lips, her tongue worming between and exploring her mouth. 'Definitely kinky,' she repeated, breaking off from the breathless kiss before moving back to her twin, where she snapped the second pair of cuffs on to her own right wrist and her sister's left.

'Mmm, kinky,' her twin agreed.

Erica decided to call the man enjoying her breasts Master A, and the other man Master B. There would be another thirteen men arriving, so she would try to allocate a letter for each one, though she knew deep down she would not remember who was called what.

'May I?' Master A asked Grace, his fingers hovering at the top of his trouser zip.

'Be my guest,' Grace told him. 'Just remember what I asked you and save plenty for later.'

He smirked, pulling down the zip and reaching inside. 'But of course, my dear host.'

When it emerged from the confines of his trousers, his cock was not fully erect, but he pulled Erica's face to it anyway. She obediently opened her mouth to accept it, and at least he smelled and tasted fresh and clean. She didn't suck at first, just existing there as he held her face still and moved his cock slowly in and out across her tongue. As he moved it grew steadily inside her mouth, slowly stretching her lips wider.

'She's good, Grace,' he said, his voice sounding slightly strained. 'Very good indeed.'

'I know,' Grace smiled. 'That's why I bought her.'

'How much to sell her again?' Master B asked.

Erica tensed involuntarily. With Grace she was reasonably contented. The cruelty was manageable. Better the devil she knew.

'That scared her,' Master A sniggered, noticing her reaction to the question, his cock pulsing in her throat.

'She's not for sale,' Grace said, a clear determination in her voice.

'Not at any price?' Master B continued.

'Not at any price,' Grace affirmed. 'Just be grateful you get to use her tonight.'

'And abuse her?' Master B asked.

'That too,' Grace agreed.

Master A was thrusting faster now and breathing more heavily. Erica knew Grace did not want him to come yet, but who was she to stop him? She flickered her eyes questioningly to where her Mistress watched.

'Remember my favour,' Grace cut in, and he began to slow his movements.

'Ah, yes,' he sighed. 'Until later, then.' Erica realised the last comment was to her.

'You really should try her,' Master A said to his twin as he pulled from her mouth and zipped up, and Master B stepped forward without any further prompting.

Within moments Erica received what felt like an identical cock in her mouth, pushed much more forcefully to the back of her throat, causing her to gag slightly. He held her head, his fingers entwined in her hair, pushing deeper until her lips were being brushed by his pubic hair and he growled with sadistic delight.

'That's enough,' Grace told him after a few minutes. 'Save it for later, remember?'

'I'll enjoy drowning you!' he hissed quietly at Erica as he pulled her roughly off his cock by her hair, leaving her kneeling on the carpet, breathing heavily from the exertion of having to suck two large erections into her throat.

The two men turned their attentions to their partners, enjoying the fact they were now cuffed together at the wrist. Grace came across to Erica and crouched down.

'You don't like my friends do you, 51?' she asked, and then added, 'I want an honest answer, remember.'

'No, Mistress.' Erica knew the men would hear, but surely that was Grace's intention anyway. 'I don't much.'

Noises from the hallway signalled the arrival of more guests. Grace went to greet them and they gradually filtered into the room. Erica noticed that two of the slaves from *The Complex* had arrived too, dressed in loose chains and minuscule black underwear. They served drinks and tried not to look at Erica. She, meanwhile, looked for the numbers on their buttocks, surprised to see that one girl was marked 102. Her tattoo looked fairly recent, and that meant they had enslaved over fifty girls since she had been taken.

The guests, too, did not take more than a passing interest in Erica, milling round chatting, enjoying drinks and canapés. Occasionally one or two would gather round her, commenting on her manner of dress or her body. One man told his companion to raise her skirt, leaving her displaying the tops of her stockings and her thong to all.

When people had eaten and had some drinks Grace called the room to order. Quickly the conversation died down so she could be heard.

'My friends,' she started, 'you all know why I've invited you here. I want to indulge myself by watching my slave 51 being used as your plaything. And she will acquiesce, because she has no will. She will acquiesce because she does what I tell her to do. Isn't that correct, 51?'

Erica was surprised she was to be included in such an announcement, even though there was only one possible answer. 'Um, yes... yes, Mistress.'

'Prove it,' said one of the men, and others joined in with the demand.

Grace stood proud in front of her guests. 'Any suggestions as to how we do that?'

There were mutters, but no suggestions at first.

'Tell her to suck every cock in the room,' a quiet female voice eventually suggested. Erica knew she would not like that woman.

'Then every pussy,' a man added.

'Very well,' Grace smiled, unfazed. '51, you heard what is expected of you.'

Erica settled on her knees uneasily, the cuffs biting into her wrists as she prepared herself.

'Free the poor girl's hands,' a man suggested, smirking. 'She can't undo zips and rub cocks like that!'

Grace produced the keys from the chain around her neck and unfastened the cuffs as Erica waited. When she was free she stood and walked to the nearest man, where she knelt down again and reached for his zip. Over the next few minutes she crawled from one to the next, unzipping and sucking until Grace told her to move on to the next. Some were already erect when she exposed them and some grew in her mouth. Two did not get erect at all, causing much amusement among the other guests and embarrassed excuses from the men themselves, and one, a fair-haired man in his early twenties, exploded into her mouth after just a few deep, tormenting sucks.

Then it was the turn of the women. Some accepted her readily, others declined. Erica kept on performing as ordered until her jaw ached from the effort, and when she had dutifully sucked all the guests she knelt head-bowed, swallowing repeatedly to come to terms with the earthy taste of the men and the juices of the women.

'Well?' Grace asked at last. 'What do you think of her?'

'She's pretty special, Grace,' said one of the men.

'I think it's only fair,' Grace continued, 'that since 51 made David come so quickly he should give her a whipping to warm her up for the main event. Does everyone agree? David?'

The general consensus was of concurrence, though most quite obviously fancied the task themselves.

Grace moved to Erica and helped her to her feet, taking her to the nearest wall. Erica had been whipped there before, so she knew what to expect. Two marble pillars were set a few feet away from the wall, and to innocent eyes they would look like ostentatious decoration, but as Grace looped a rope several times round Erica's right wrist, it was obvious to all concerned that the pillars had a much more erotic significance than mere ornamentation. When Grace had finished tying the rope she stood on a stool to attach its other end high up the pillar, where the profile of the carving made sure it would not slip down.

Erica was aware that her mistress had pulled the rope tighter than she usually did, and when the second rope was tied, pulling her left arm high up the second pillar, she had to stand on tiptoe to ease the strain.

Grace unfastened the halter, so that the dress floated down Erica's curves, catching briefly on the suspender belt then slipping noiselessly to the floor. Someone, male by the feel of it, tapped her ankles to indicate she should step out of it. Then more ropes were fastened to her ankles. She tried to look down to check what was happening but could not get the angle to see, but from what she could feel the ankle ropes had been passed round the base of each pillar.

'David, would you care to select a whip?' Grace asked from nearby.

Erica heard the drawers of the cabinet being opened, a tense air of anticipation settling over the room.

There was more movement just behind her, and Erica felt the ropes at her ankles being pulled towards each pillar, toppling her from her tiptoe position, her feet being pulled wide apart, meaning they could not support her weight any longer and her bound wrists had to take all the strain. Her breath left her lungs as she was held taut by the ropes stretching her arms upward; her feet now pulled uselessly a couple of inches from the floor.

'I think we're ready,' Grace announced, and Erica tensed. She sensed David behind her, watching her tense with dread, choosing his moment to lash out... and when it came it made her cry out. She did not want to, she wanted to show these people she was every bit as determined as they were, that she was not merely some feeble toy they could use and then discard when they got bored.

After three strokes she realised David was a novice with the whip. His aim was bad and the usual bite of the tip - the action that caused most pain and damage - was missing from his technique.

Then a girl appeared in front of her - David's partner, from what Erica could ascertain. The white dress she wore emphasised her tan and the outline of her erect nipples. She sipped champagne, eyeing Erica's expression as each stroke landed. She reached out slowly and slipped her fingers inside Erica's thong, pressing them between the wet pussy lips they found there.

'She's really enjoying it,' the girl announced. 'She's soaking wet. You are enjoying this, aren't you, 51?'

'No, Mistress,' Erica replied honestly.

'I don't believe you, slave, and now it's time you had a proper whipping.'

She moved from Erica's limited field of vision, and the strokes from David ceased for a few moments as he handed the whip to her. The next stroke make Erica scream afresh, lashing down her tensed back, the flick of the tip doing its job perfectly. Then the girl's face appeared again.

'Do you know what I used to do as a profession, 51?' she asked.

'N-no, Mistress, how could I?' Erica sobbed.

'I used to be in a circus, perfecting tricks with a whip just like this one. I could whip a cigarette from between your lips without touching you. And now I'm going to take that thong off you. Enjoy and admire my skills, slave.'

The pain, the crack and Erica's shriek almost coincided as the tip of the whip flicked at the upper slope of her right buttock, where the string of her thong traversed it. Erica prayed it had given, but it had not, and she knew more was to come. It took three strokes to cut through the thin strip and the murmur of approval was all that was needed to signal it had given.

'And now the other side,' she heard the woman say, and Erica braced herself again. The sadistic female took her time between strokes, but again on the third Erica felt the tattered thong flop between her legs, pause there for a moment, and then drop to the carpet. The strain of her forced position and the pain from the whip made her feel lightheaded and the wall in front of her started to drift and slowly spin. Then from somewhere beyond the haze that started to engulf her she heard Grace say, 'Help me get her down.'

Erica was only vaguely aware of the hands that untied and supported her from between the pillars to a sofa. She was allowed to rest for a while as the guests enjoyed more food and drink, and in her vision stood the ominous metal frame, waiting for her.

CHAPTER 17

Erica wondered where she was for those few moments when the subconscious refuses to allow reality to rule, but as her eyes focussed on the frame she remembered all too well. She closed her eyes again and sensed Grace's presence from her perfume, moments before she felt the hand on her shoulder.

'It's time, 51,' her voice said, as Erica cautiously opened her eyes. 'Stand up now.'

Grace led Erica to the frame and positioned her so that her back was against the central bar. She flinched as the cold steel touched her hot flesh and Grace tightened the strap around her waist. With David's help she fastened Erica's wrists to the straps on the arms of the unit, and then her ankles and knees to the vertical supports. A strap just under her breasts held her firm against the frame and the final straps around her throat and forehead stopped any movement other than that permitted by the lockable joints of the frame itself.

Grace carefully arranged the joints so Erica's legs were apart by about two feet, and then locked her arms in position at a similar angle. Once fixed they rotated the frame back to a horizontal position so that all Erica could see was the ceiling, and anyone who cared to wander into her restricted field of vision.

Grace produced a rubber dental clamp and pushed it between Erica's teeth, fixing her mouth wide open.

Grace then called for attention. 'Ladies and gentlemen, we come to the point I invited you all here for. I would like to see my slave completely defiled, covered from head to toe in your emissions. There's no part of her that's off limits. She is my object, my complete property and I want her debased to the lowest level. Take your time, my friends, and use her as you wish. For the moment, at least, I give you my slave, 51.'

There was no great rush to accept Grace's generosity, as if nobody wanted to be the first to move, but it came as no surprise to Erica that the woman who had taken great delight in whipping her started the action, appearing naked above Erica's head, staring down at her.

'I'm going to own you one day,' she hissed in her ear, so the rest of the room would not hear. 'And I'll be much more cruel than Grace is.' She raised her voice to address the onlookers. 'Well, any takers? I have two very talented hands here.' She held up beautifully manicured fingers, as if to confirm her claim. 'I just need a couple of you men to help me prove it and bathe this slut in spunk.'

Erica could not see what happened next, but gathered from what she could hear that some men were moving close. She could not see their faces; she did not want to see their faces. They could use and abuse her body, but they would never own her soul. Not really.

The woman reached for the man to her right and drew down the trouser zip of his grey suit, tugging his semi-erect cock out into view. It dangled there, pointing at Erica's ensnared face, as the woman turned her attention to the man to her left, unzipping his black slacks with equal deftness. He was a little more erect than the first, but the woman soon had both men rising proudly as she caressed and rubbed their cocks with one fist enveloping each. Watching Erica's eyes, she dipped her head low to suck in the first man, then sucked in the second, alternating between them and leaving them glistening with her saliva.

'Now, pretty one,' she growled quietly, 'let's see how you look covered in their spunk...'

She started to pump both men in unison as Erica could do nothing but watch from beneath. They were quickly groaning and uttering crudities, thrusting into the woman's artful hands as she pumped them. Then Erica was distracted and dismayed when a third man joined in, moving between her legs and rubbing his already bloated helmet between her vulnerable sex lips.

The man to her left suddenly grunted throatily, turning Erica's attention back to him as a copious spurt of sticky seed splattered from the tip of his pulsing erection. The calculating woman aimed with intent so that the first eruption coated Erica's lips and seeped into her mouth, then used the flagging cock to spread it over her face, as though spreading some fruit preserve onto a scone. When the man had almost stopped pumping the woman fed his cock into Erica's mouth, where it dribbled its last few viscous drops onto her tongue. With the rubber wedge between her teeth and her head held fast, Erica had no choice but to swallow.

Perhaps spurred on by the sight of her taking the first man's emission, the second was not far behind. As he drew close the woman released her grip to take some of Erica's hair, wrapping it around the man's erection, to be rewarded seconds later by several gushes of sperm oozing into it.

'I need a drink,' the woman eventually said, disdainfully releasing the two spent cocks and disappearing from Erica's very limited view.

The man between Erica's legs was pushing slightly into her; just far enough to get his thrills and watch her discomfort. Another man appeared at her side, naked, his erection in his right hand while his left arm was draped around the shoulders of a topless girl, the hand dropping far enough to cup her breast. Looking down at Erica he wanked furiously, soon showering her breasts and belly with gouts of warm, gluey come.

The man between her legs lodged his helmet between her pussy lips, pumping the stem of his cock in his fist, and then eventually pulling out to spatter his seed into the gentle dip of her quivering tummy. When it cooled it trickled disgustingly down over her hip, but since she could not move there was nothing she could do.

A strikingly attractive blonde girl pulled her man into position, leaning across Erica and sucking him within inches of her face, taking him deep until he started to lose control. As he came she pulled away and directed the stream onto Erica's face, who noticed Grace in the corner of her vision, watching excitedly.

Her mistress had apparently selected her guests carefully. Two men were seriously into feet, rubbing their erections against hers until they spurted over them. Some were after her breasts, until they too were dripping with come. Two came inside her pussy, rutting and swearing as they ejaculated.

One insisted the frame should be spun over so he could penetrate her arse, where he fucked vigorously until he finished, with a stream of crude expletives aimed at the bound slave. When she was turned back over she could feel his chilling seed dripping from her.

But by far the most popular target was her mouth and face. They came and came again, until she was completely covered and had no idea how much she had swallowed. She could barely see through a glistening, glutinous coating that covered her eyes. At one point an erect cock was placed in each of her hands and she obediently pumped them until she felt the seed dribble between her fingers.

Occasionally some women would join in, either by coaxing their men to a climax, aiming at Erica's face or body or hair, or by taking their own pleasure from her fingers. Each time she would use her trained hands to stroke and coax and bring them off if she could. One woman wanted to mount her face, but Grace refused her, wanting to leave her features as messy as could be.

Erica lost track of how long she was there, only that she felt disgustingly filthy. Her hair felt worst of all, matted and sticky with male ejaculate, although the rest of her weary body felt as if it had drying glue on it.

Finally she was released. She desperately wanted to shower, to rid herself of their filthy excesses, and then to curl up in a soft bed and sleep. She had accepted and endured the ordeal, and felt triumphant for it, because now nothing stood in the way of her date with her stepfather and his with destiny.

CHAPTER 18

Saturday could not come soon enough for Erica. Grace outlined the plan again and again. There was no way the management of *The Complex* would permit it, so Grace had selected two men who were good friends and would assist without any recriminations.

After dark on Saturday they would bring one of *The Complex's* limousines to Grace's house and they would get in, with Erica in the boot for two reasons: firstly, nobody apart from the two of them and the two men must know they ever left *The Complex*, and secondly that Erica must have no clue as to where *The Complex* was.

Grace wanted to know everything Erica could remember about her parents' house, including detailed descriptions of all the rooms and the grounds, plus any knowledge of alarms, neighbours, pets, locks, habits and so on. She made copious notes as Erica spoke, altering her plans at each relevant piece of information. When it was all finished Grace told Erica what she proposed, including the way she would kill her stepfather.

Erica slept very well each night. Until it was Friday. She hardly slept at all on Friday night. Grace probably realised she would be tense, so she strapped Erica to her bed and spent a long time sucking her pussy, as much for her own excitement as Erica's.

On the Saturday itself both females did all they could to help time to pass quickly, and at last it was dark when the two men arrived, dressed all in black as if they were on some secret SAS mission. It almost made Erica smile at the theatrical way this was unfolding, until she realised that it was quite possible these men were SAS, or ex-SAS. They certainly moved with stealth as if they knew exactly what they were doing.

Grace was also dressed fully in black. It was the first time Erica had ever seen her dressed in trousers, but she was not allowed the same freedom. Grace had selected a very seductive outfit with black underwear - a thong, suspenders, seamed stockings - and a tiny black dress slit to the thigh on both sides, its bustier top holding Erica's breasts firmly in place while making them look as if they would spill out with the slightest encouragement. Erica did not want to ask why the others were dressed appropriately while she looked as if she was attending a sexy cocktail party, and she did not need to as Grace decided to explain.

'From what you told me, your stepfather has an eye for the women, yes?' she asked.

Erica nodded.

'Well, you could just go in and shoot him, just like that. But wouldn't you like to show him, one last time, what he's about to lose? Don't you want to show him that he thought he could possess you, sexy, feisty Erica, but you've got the final victory?'

'Yes, oh yes,' Erica said. She loved the idea. She would taunt him and make him squirm. Then she would have her ultimate revenge for everything he had put her through.

Erica's heels clicked on the paving as they led her out to the car. The large boot was already open, waiting for her, a feather duvet across the width of it. One of the men picked her up as if she weighed nothing and lowered her onto it. Grace appeared with ropes, wrapping one several times round her wrists in front of her and securing them to the framework at the left side of the car boot. Another rope tied her feet together and to the framework at the right side. A third rope, as if it was necessary, tied her knees together. Grace pushed a ball gag between her lips and fastened the straps.

'See you later, slave,' she smiled down as the man closed the boot lid.

Erica watched as darkness enfolded her, the only illumination coming from the interior light of the car's boot, but when it was almost shut that went out too. She tried to imagine the journey as the car started and moved smoothly off. She could tell when it moved left and right. She heard gravel under the wheels for a few hundred yards. If she could remember the route and recognise where they emerged maybe, just maybe, she could lead the authorities back here one day. If she could find any authorities who were not a part of it all, that is. She had to believe she could, just as she had to believe that someday, somehow, she would escape.

Erica estimated they travelled for fifteen minutes before they stopped. She waited, since she could do nothing else, for them to come and free her from the boot, trying to make out words from the muffled voices within the car. But the soundproofing was too effective to hear clearly.

After a few minutes she heard the doors opening and footsteps making their way round. For some reason she expected to be blinded by lights when the boot lid opened, but outside was very dark. Until, that is, one of the men shone a torch straight into her face, and she was almost grateful when Grace fitted a blindfold on her. She felt her wrists being untied from the car and her legs being released, and then she was lifted clear from the boot.

She was unsteady on her feet at first and had to be supported, but when she could stand there was a tug on the rope and she was being pulled forward across solid ground, half walking, half running, her heels clicking on what felt like a concrete surface. Then she was being lifted into another vehicle, one that echoed and was big enough so that she could stand up in it without banging her head.

Her wrists were untied for a moment, but only long enough to have leather straps fitted around them. She heard locks snap in place before her arms were being pulled upwards and outwards, fastened to anchors above and to each side, stretching her out and holding her upright. When her arms were fastened they put straps around her ankles too, eventually pulling them wide apart, holding her in a vertical X shape.

When they suddenly removed the blindfold Erica saw that she was inside a van. The rear doors were open behind her, but when she turn to try to see any signs of where she was, the torch shone right in her face again. Ahead of her was the front of the compartment, with no view through to the cab to give her any clues.

Then Grace was by her side again. 'Are you ready for this?' she asked. 'Still want to go through with it?'

Erica took a deep breath. 'Yes, Mistress,' she said.

'One of my friends thinks you'll benefit from a reminder of what your stepfather committed you to,' Grace told her, already tugging the dress up and tucking it into her suspender belt. Then she stepped away and Erica felt the van shift as she climbed out. A moment later the whip cracked across her backside, making her scream out loud and arch her back away from the pain.

One of the men was almost immediately beside her again, binding some kind of leather belt around her waist and attaching straps to the van's sides, and Erica found she could not move her hips at all once they were fastened, so this time when the whip lashed out there was no way to arch away from it. Five more times it bit into her and each time she yelped out in pain. If their idea was to get her adrenalin going for the task ahead, it was certainly effective. She could feel once more the driving need to get even with the man who had her condemned to a life of slavery. And as for her mother, how could she stand by and commit her own daughter to what she'd had to endure?

The doors slammed, leaving Erica alone. She heard both of the cabin doors shut before the engine started, and they were off, driving fast and smoothly down meandering roads. Erica had no choice other than to hang on to her bonds, adjusting her weight as best she could as the van twisted its way towards her revenge.

In a desperate effort to guess the approximate whereabouts of *The Complex*, as the van came to a halt, Erica estimated their travelling time at a little less than an hour, though she had no real idea how fast the van had been moving. She felt as if she was in familiar surroundings, more of an incomprehensible sixth sense than any clue she could define. Then she heard the faint squeak - the automatic gates of the house she grew up in! At last she had arrived back home, and a quick mental calculation told her *The Complex* was probably only about thirty to forty miles away, though she had no idea in which direction.

The gravel of the driveway crunched beneath the van's wheels as it slowly made its way towards the house and drew to a halt. Erica listened intently as the van's doors opened and closed quietly, so as to conceal their arrival for as long as possible. Two sets of footsteps receded stealthily towards the house. Erica was not sure if Grace was still in the van, but she could do little except wait.

About ten minutes later she heard footsteps again, except this time they were heavier, as if stealth were no longer required. The rear doors of the van opened again and Grace climbed in to untie her, first her ankles, then her waist, and finally her wrists. She snapped a leash into the ring on Erica's collar and turned to leave the van. Through the open doors Erica saw once again the features of the gardens of her home, illuminated by the floodlights set in the lawns.

Grace jumped down from the van, assisted by one of the men, pulling Erica behind her. It was then that Erica noticed the gun tucked in his waistband. The second man was nowhere to be seen.

Grace led her to the open front door of her old house. Erica felt cold and emotionless; she had often imagined coming back here, either as a free person or with a score to settle, as now. It felt strange returning to the house she had once known so well. It was familiar, yet at the same time so unreal. Erica climbed the three stone steps to the front door and went in, the leash dangling behind her. Inside the hall lights sent eerie shadows across the walls - her parents never did like strong lighting.

Then it was left, to the library door. As Grace pushed it open Erica saw her stepfather sitting in the leather chair in front of his desk, and her pulse started to quicken. The lights were low in here too, only the MP's desk lamp illuminating the tense scene. He did not look at her as she entered; instead he stared at the pistol the second man was pointing at his chest. They moved forward, towards him.

'Erica!' The exclamation came from their right. In the shadows, sitting on a high-backed dining chair was her mother, looking terrified. Her arms had been tied behind her and her ankles were bound together.

'Hello, Mother,' Erica said coldly, her face expressionless.

'Take her away,' Grace told one of the men, nodding at Erica's mother, and Erica watched without feeling as he untied her, picked her up and carried her out of the room, everyone ignoring her pleas for leniency.

'If this is some kind of joke, young lady—' Laurence Pettinger started to say, but Grace stepped forward and slapped him hard across the face with the back of her hand.

'Silence!' she hissed.

He looked up at her slowly. 'I know you,' he said. 'You're...'

'I said silence!' Grace growled, striking him again, the impact snapping his head to the other side.

The other man returned to the room and nodded to Grace, who walked back to Erica and unfastened the leash. 'We have some special rules tonight,' she explained to her. 'My associates both have guns, and if you make any attempt to escape they will stop you. Do you understand me?'

Erica nodded obediently. She was not going anywhere... not yet. This moment was far too important to her.

'Good.' Grace smiled knowingly. 'But apart from that you may do pretty much as you please. He wronged you, and now at last here's your chance to get your own back. I'll provide anything you want.' She stepped back, allowing Erica to move in front of her stepfather.

'Stand up,' she told him. He looked up at her, but did not move. Erica glanced towards Grace, who nodded to her nearest male accomplice. He moved to the sitting man and pressed the gun to his temple.

'I'd advise you to do exactly as your daughter says,' he threatened coldly.

'I'm not his daughter,' Erica snapped with pent up venom.

The man turned to stare at her. 'Just because you're at home does not mean you have any rights, *slave*,' he warned, and Erica flinched; nothing must ruin her moment of vengeance.

'I'm sorry, Master,' she said meekly.

125

'And you, do as she says,' the man said again, turning his attention back to Laurence Pettinger and pressing the gun harder against his temple.

Suddenly the pressure seemed to get to Erica's stepfather and he crumbled visibly, his shoulders sagging as he gingerly stood up, keeping a wary eye on the man with the gun, who retreated to lean his hips against the edge of the desk, the gun still trained on its target. Erica watched, thinking how pathetic her stepfather now looked. All that austere arrogance, yet now he was a quivering coward. But she still felt not a shred of sympathy for him.

She walked close to him, stared him in the eye, and then kneed him in the groin, making him crumple back into the leather chair. Then swaying slowly to imaginary music, the way a lap-dancer would, Erica leaned towards him and ran her right hand sexily through her hair, enticing him with her shadowy cleavage.

'Do you want me?' she purred seductively, seeing his lecherous eyes unable to resist taking a peep at the smoothness of the upper slopes of her breasts, despite the predicament he was in.

'Erica, I—'

'Nobody said you could speak, slave!' she spat, slapping him hard across the face. Then immediately she was softer again, renewing her swaying, cupping her breasts, turning her back to entice him with the glorious shape of her bottom.

Then suddenly, unable to control his lusty urges, Laurence Pettinger grabbed for her. It bundled Erica off balance and she fell onto him, but the nearest man moved swiftly from his post against the desk, his fist smashing into Pettinger's face, knocking him sideways and allowing Erica to recover and pull from his clutches.

'Don't try that again,' the man spat. 'She's not yours to use any more. Anyone else's, but not yours.'

And then to emphasise his point the man unzipped his trousers and withdrew an erection that put her stepfather's to shame. He pushed Erica's shoulder until she bent forward slightly, then lifted her skirt and bent his legs to allow him an angle to callously feed that column of throbbing flesh into her.

'I can fuck you, 51, can't I?' he said through gritted teeth. 'I can use you in any way I want, can't I?'

'Yes, Master, anything,' she panted back, her eyes closing as his cock stretched her.

'And can he fuck you, 51?' the man goaded.

Erica shook her head, her moist lips parting as a shunt of his hips caused her to gasp softly.

'Any man in the world can have you, except your stepfather?'

Erica nodded dreamily. 'Yes, Master.'

The man twisted his hand in her hair, pulling her back against him as he fucked her from behind, aggressively stabbing his cock into her, the pistol still in his free hand. 'Anyone but you, Laurence Pettinger, MP,' he mocked.

'What have I ever done to you?' Laurence whimpered, gingerly touching his fingertips to his already swelling lower lip. 'What?'

126

The man ignored him, pulling away from Erica and resuming his position against the desk, the gun trained on its target still.

Erica took a few moments to compose herself. Laurence Pettinger could not fail to be entranced by her, but then again he always was, back to when she was a precocious teenager living at home. She was dancing again, right in front of him, then Grace's voice cut into the electric atmosphere. 'Are you ready, Erica?' she asked, and Erica stopped dancing for a moment, nodding tentatively.

Grace spoke to the second man, who advanced on Laurence Pettinger. From his pocket he pulled a pair of handcuffs and, after pulling the captive roughly to his feet, he snapped them onto his wrists so his hands were locked behind his back. From somewhere the other man had produced a heavy rope, coiled as if prepared beforehand. As he tossed it to his associate it uncoiled slightly, and the second man roped the MP's ankles together while the first handed Erica a dark, sinister shape, and it was not until she turned to face her stepfather that he saw it was another gun.

'Oh God, n-no!' he stammered. 'Erica, please, you can't...'

'One shot, 51,' the man told her, ignoring the blubbering of her stepfather. 'That's all you have in there. And if you try anything clever...' He did not need to finish his threat. The gun he now had trained on her heart said it for him, so Erica turned her focus back to her stepfather.

'You took my life away,' she said, her tone strangely emotionless. 'I'll never be free again; somehow I've come to accept that. But because of you... because of your devious cruelty... my life doesn't belong to me any more. So if I can't have my own life, because of you, you're not going to have your life either.'

'Erica...' he mumbled pitifully.

'I think that's only fair. Don't you?'

'Erica, please no...' Laurence Pettinger, MP, sank to his knees. 'You want me to say I'm sorry? Is that what you want? Then I'll say it. I'm sorry, Erica, really I am.'

'Too late,' was Erica's simple response.

'I can get you freed,' he suddenly gabbled desperately. 'I have influence.'

'Will I ever be freed, Mistress?' Erica asked, not taking her eyes off the grovelling, pitiful man kneeling before her. 'Can he promise me that?'

'No, Erica,' Grace replied gently. 'There's nothing he can do for you.'

'Please, I'm begging!' He leaned forward, toppling onto the floor with no arms to support him, snivelling at Erica's feet, trying to kiss them in some pathetic, belated attempt at appeasement. 'Please, please Erica,' he babbled over and over.

Erica lifted her foot, pressing the point of her stiletto heel down into his cheek until he was gasping in agony. She should have felt remorse. She was glad she felt none.

The lurking man moved to Laurence and lifted him back into the chair, while he surprised Erica by seemingly recovering some strength and defiance. She looked at her stepfather, and he stared back up at her, his head tilted slightly to one side.

'OK, young lady, you've had your moment,' he said. 'Now let me go, there's a good girl. I'll come to *The Complex* tomorrow and bring you home.'

Erica pouted at him. 'But can't I stay here at home now?' she asked. 'Why send me back there only to come and get me again in the morning?'

Laurence Pettinger faltered. 'Yes, yes... that's what I meant,' he stumbled.

'And will we have fun together, when I'm back home?' she coaxed suggestively.

He was unsure how to answer. 'Ah, anything you want.'

Whether he thought she was actually going to release him or not, she could not tell. Maybe fear had convinced him that this was all a vengeful joke, that it was inconceivable that it could go any further.

But Erica was enjoying herself.

Erica was making the moment last.

Erica slowly lifted the pistol, surprised at its weight. Laurence stared, speechless now, his eyes fixed on the small circular hole of the barrel. Nobody in that room was going to help him. He was already dead.

She stared at him, so focussed that everything else receded from her consciousness. They had never before been this close; never before had this intensity of communication. She had no idea how long the silent moment lasted, and then a tear trickling down his cheek broke the spell.

Erica raised the pistol a little more and pointed at her stepfather's forehead. She had never fired a gun before but she was confident that at this range she would not fail herself. 'Squeeze the trigger, don't pull.' Wasn't that what they always said on TV?

Erica squeezed. She didn't pull. The explosion of noise deafened her and the bright glare was like lightning. In slow motion she watched a small hole appear in the centre of her stepfather's forehead. He didn't move, and she thought she must have missed in some way. He was still there, staring at her. Still alive. Damn him!

This time she pulled, and all she got was a click. But it didn't matter. Laurence Pettinger's head fell forward and his slack chin lolled on his chest. A trickle of blood seeped from the wound. She expected more. She felt cheated that there wasn't more.

Then there were noises from in the room. Tense breathing. People.

Erica turned to face them. The men were silent. Grace was lurking in the shadows, hardly visible apart from a tiny red light where her face should be, and it was then that Erica realised the entire scene had been captured on a video camera. 'W-what...?' she started.

'Insurance,' Grace stated frankly, lowering the camera a little. 'Now you're mine forever.' The red light went out as she moved forward. 'Right, time to go,' she said, addressing her two accomplices rather than Erica. 'Tie her again, ready for the journey.'

Erica stood hopelessly still as the men roped her arms and legs together until she could not move.

'What about...?' She meant her mother, just before a strip of tape was smoothed across her mouth.

'No loose ends,' the taller man said, and Erica screamed behind the gag as the other man nodded at his male accomplice and silently left the room - clearly intent on finishing the job.

www.ingramcontent.com/pod-product-compliance
Lightning Source LLC
Chambersburg PA
CBHW020409130626
46549CB00006B/2499